Her grandmoth[...]
her to her side.

She kissed Carrie's hand. From under the pillow on her bed, she took out the velvet bag.

"Carrie, my dearest, I want you to have this. It will be a secret between you and me." She slipped the box with its key out of the bag. "My precious husband gave this to me on our wedding day. He said it represented the key to his heart and that I possessed it forever and ever. Wasn't that a wonderful thing to say? And each year until his death, he reminded me of that promise.

"Now, listen to me and remember. Will you?" Carrie nodded, and her grandmother continued. "When you grow up, I want you to marry a romantic man like your grandfather." She took a deep breath. "Wait, Carrie. Wait until the right man comes along. God will send him. You just wait."

FREDA CHRISMAN is the author of one novella and three books. Prior to publishing her first novel with **Heartsong Presents,** Freda's articles and short stories appeared in Sunday school take-home papers and denominational magazines. She lives in the Houston metroplex.

Books by Freda Chrisman

HEARTSONG PRESENTS
HP233—Faith Came Late
HP404—At the Golden Gate

Two Hearts Wait

Freda Chrisman

Heartsong Presents

With gratitude to Rebecca Germany and to the Texans of Inspirational Writers Alive!

A note from the author:
I love to hear from my readers! You may correspond with me by writing:

Freda Chrisman
Author Relations
PO Box 719
Uhrichsville, OH 44683

ISBN 1-58660-769-3

TWO HEARTS WAIT

All Scripture quotations are taken from the King James Version of the Bible.

PRINTED IN THE U.S.A.

one

Maryland, 1850

"Carrie, you are being too severe on Papa!" cried her older sister. "He is thinking only of your best interests."

Carrie Warden's dainty cup and saucer clattered as she dumped them on her mother's polished mahogany table. Tea splashed wildly over the edge of the cup, and she winced. Mama was occupied in her sitting room. If she saw her favorite bone china so near disaster, she'd fall into a fit of vapors, Carrie reasoned uneasily.

"Why are you so cruel to me, Virgie?" she asked. "Your own baby sister. Alfred Rafter is old! He's nearly fifty! How can you push me toward marriage with such a man? His face always looks as if he's sucking a lemon."

"Carrie, what an unladylike expression." Virgie laid her delicate embroidery in her lap and deftly refilled her cup from the silver service next to her chair. Her back straight as a plumb line, she sipped her tea, then brushed at a fold in her dark blue morning gown.

Through tight lips, she chided, "You should not use such a hateful tone with me, Carrie. I'm only trying to help. Yes, you're pretty. You have beautiful brown eyes and hair like sunshine. But those things are not important.

"You are nineteen, beyond time for you to marry. Papa has made a most suitable match for you." Obviously satisfied she'd created the right atmosphere, Virgie pressed on. "I'm trying to make you aware of the rare opportunity this is for you."

Virgie set her tea on the table. "Carrie, think! Just think what Mr. Rafter's vast shipping business will mean to your future and to that of your offspring. You will want for nothing. He is a very wealthy man."

Eyes blazing, Carrie marched to stand in front of her sister. "I would want for nothing? Do you consider warmth, companionship, and compatibility nothing?" She spread her small hands before Virgie. "How can you disregard them? And love? I want to marry for love, not simply to please Papa or you. I intend to wait for a proper husband! Do you hear me? I intend to wait!"

"You are too strong-willed, Carrie. You should consider yourself fortunate that Papa has chosen such a man for you. Instead of riding the fields every minute you can get away, you should be creating a stack of superb linen for the great house of which you will be mistress one day."

Virgie's voice turned morose. "Mama taught you well in the art of housekeeping, but your sewing is abominable. You must spend less time on that horse of yours and practice your needlework instead." She closed her eyes. "Papa says you have the heart of a vagabond. He believes you need a man who will settle you down and teach you the gentle art of domesticity." She stabbed

Carrie with a look. "I agree completely."

Carrie kicked the skirt of her forest green riding habit out of the way and dropped awkwardly between the arms of a Hepplewhite chair. "Virginia Mae, how can you be so insensitive? Encouraging Papa to marry me off to that old man against my will!" she taunted, addressing her sister with the name she despised.

Ignoring her remarks, Virgie continued to haggle. "You spoke of a proper husband. What sort of man do you consider a proper husband, if I may ask? I married when Papa found the right man for me, and as you know, Conrad and I are perfectly matched." Her tight lips relaxed only slightly.

"You do exactly what Conrad wants you to do, just as you did with Papa. That's why you are perfectly matched," Carrie spat. Leaning forward, she captured Virgie's gaze. "Have you no pity for me? Do you want me to end up in a loveless marriage like yours?"

Carrie knew she was being unfair. But if she didn't take a stand for herself, the pressure to marry Alfred Rafter would increase.

Her auburn hair drawn back into a tight bun at her neck, Virgie turned a pale face and riveting brown eyes toward Carrie. "How cruel of you to criticize what has been a very satisfactory alliance." Sipping her tea, then setting it down again, Virgie attacked her embroidery as if it were an enemy.

Carrie lowered her gaze and picked at a fingernail. She knew she should apologize. Maybe her sister did have a pleasant married life. Maybe her husband was not as demanding as he seemed. Maybe he treated Virgie differently when they were at home. Maybe.

"I'm sorry, Virgie. I had no right to criticize your marriage. Yet, neither should you criticize my wish to avoid that state of blessedness, as you call it. There are things I'd like to do before I settle down."

She caught Virgie's glare of disapproval. "I know, we each had our schooling with Miss Stimson, and I'm grateful Papa was open-minded enough to send us. Some young ladies, however, are going further with their studies. There are finishing schools that teach—"

"Carrie Elizabeth Warden! Don't you dare mention such a thing to Papa!" Virgie jumped to her feet, red-faced but resolved. With a wilting tone of censure, she declared, "I can see there is nothing to do but talk to Mother. Where do you get such wild ideas? Finishing schools, indeed!"

Virgie picked up her embroidery, stuffed it into her sewing basket, and stamped across the oak floor of the parlor toward the hall. "I'll have a word with Mother. Maybe when she talks to you, you'll come to your senses. Later, we will speak again."

Slumping back in her chair, arms folded across her chest, Carrie tried to relax. She knew she should change out of her riding clothes, but the tension from her quarrel with Virgie left her yearning for a moment alone.

Her gaze roamed the parameters of the handsome room: its long, blue velvet drapes at the tall windows, the mahogany chairs and comfortable couches, a matching mahogany desk and étagère, a tall wooden clock, a huge bay window. It was the kind of home she wanted someday. But not yet.

She knew there was little chance of continuing her education. She had dreamed of extending her studies with a tutor because she had heard of a girl whose papa had actually hired one.

Traveling on her own was another desire. She smiled. What would Virgie have said if she had mentioned travel? For two years she had begged to go to New York to visit her friend Alice Garner, but Papa would not hear of it. Not ever.

She sauntered out of the room with her riding skirt flung over her arm. In the entryway, windows on either side of the double door allowed sunshine to sweep across its ivory walls and dark walnut trim. During the day, the room radiated a bright welcome.

Carrie climbed the gracefully curved staircase to the upper floor and, at the end of the hall, opened the door to her sanctuary. Now that Virgie no longer lived at home, she had the big room all to herself. It was her domain.

She had no startling secrets hidden away, but her room was her own, and she demanded that others regard it so. She did own one thing that no one knew about, and to boost her morale, she needed to touch that love gift now.

Retrieving a small pink velvet bag from a top drawer of the lingerie chest, she carried it to her four-poster bed and sat on the quilted spread of yellow and white daisies. Ruffled white curtains coaxed sunlight into the room, and walls of yellow plaster reflected light upon the spot where she sat.

Carrie loosened the drawstring of the pink bag, and out slid a gold box. Inside lay a small gold key on a bed of pink velvet. When she was seven years old, her grandmother had shown her the key and told her a story Carrie never forgot.

Grandfather Lawrence had seen Grandmother in church and fallen in love with her immediately. Through a friend, he managed an interview with her parents, proceeded to court her, and finally married her on Christmas Day.

Carrie thought their story more romantic than the tale of Romeo and Juliet. Her grandparents had loved each other deeply, and it was their love that spurred Carrie's desire for the same kind of love in her life.

After that, Grandmother Lawrence became very ill, and Carrie was not permitted to ask questions about her health. But one day, when the others had left the room to let her grandmother rest, Carrie slipped in and stood quietly watching. Her grandmother opened her eyes and beckoned her to her side. She kissed Carrie's hand. From under the pillow on her bed, she took out the velvet bag.

"Carrie, my dearest, I want you to have this. It will be a secret between you and me." She slipped the box with its key out of the bag. "My precious husband gave this to me on our wedding day. He said it represented the key to his heart and that I possessed it forever and ever. Wasn't that a wonderful thing to say? And each year until his death, he reminded me of that promise.

"Now, listen to me and remember. Will you?" Carrie nodded, and her grandmother continued. "When you grow up, I want you to marry a romantic man like your grandfather." She took a deep breath. "Wait, Carrie. Wait until the right man comes along. God will send him. You just wait."

Grandmother Lawrence had died soon after that, and Carrie could still remember how long it had taken for her young heart to feel whole again. But she never forgot the soft, caring look on her grandmother's face when she gave Carrie the token that meant more to her than anything.

That was the reason for her quarrel with Virgie, and that was the reason she could never marry the elderly gentleman her father had selected for her. She would escape the proposed arrangement and wait as her grandmother wished.

But she did not believe God would see to it. In the Bible stories she had heard of, He was always busy with wars and battles. No, she'd better not depend on God. She would secure a proper man by herself.

It was possible. Why, only today she had caught a glimpse of an appealing man. He had galloped his black horse across her path only a hundred yards ahead. She did not recognize him, yet his stately physique and fine horsemanship impressed her. He was a good example. There were other men in the world to marry instead of a gray-haired, fifty-year-old widower!

A pounding at the door interrupted her thoughts, and her little brother, Trouble—an apt substitute for his real name, Travis—stuck his head around the door. Carrie hid her secret keepsake beneath a fold of her habit and smiled at him.

"Carrie, change your dress quick!" he exclaimed. "Papa wants you downstairs for a talk. He's very angry because you went riding when you knew Mr. Rafter was coming by the house."

Trouble's flushed face brought out the freckles covering his nose and cheeks. Smoothing unruly red curls, he swayed from side to side and watched Carrie with anxious brown eyes. She knew he awaited her reaction.

Carrie took a plain brown linen frock from her armoire. "Go down quietly, Trouble, and try not to make him any more angry. I did not want to meet Mr. Rafter today; but, please, don't tell Papa." Returning to her lingerie drawer, she placed the keepsake under her handkerchiefs and took out a cream-colored frilly collar for her dress that she hoped would make her look younger. "Scoot, Trouble!" she urged.

Hesitating, he replied, "But I wanted to talk to you."

Carrie was always ready to listen when Trouble asked. Only ten years old, he was her favorite family member. She grabbed her dress and slipped behind a gold silk screen bordered with blue cornflowers. She poured water from a pitcher into her washbasin.

"Forgive me, little man. I'm not being very considerate, am I? Talk to me while I freshen up and change."

"You're nervous about the talk with Papa. So am I. None of you will tell me what's happening, but I know anyway. You shouldn't have to marry Mr. Rafter. If Papa tries to make you, you should run away. I'll help you if you want me to."

Carrie peeked around the side of the screen. "Travis Warden, you are the sweetest brother. I'll give you a kiss when I come out."

"Well, no, you don't have to do that."

"You'd be embarrassed, wouldn't you? All right. But I do appreciate your warning me about Papa. You're giving me time to pull my thoughts together." She heard him pacing about and realized he was truly worried for her.

"What will you say?" he asked. "What excuse can you give for not marrying old Mr. Rafter?"

Her voice muffled as she pulled the brown dress over her head, and she scolded gently. "You mustn't be disrespectful, Dear." Then, in a clear voice, "I haven't the slightest intention of marrying Alfred Rafter. Before I consent to such a thing, I'll leave home and earn my own livelihood." Giggling, she added, "I shall sacrifice myself and teach ten-year-old boys spelling and arithmetic."

"I already know my spelling and arithmetic. Mr. Ellison makes sure of that," he muttered, speaking of his tutor.

Carrie came around the screen fastening the frilly

collar at her throat. "Then I must think of another route of escape. But I can assure you I will not marry Alfred Rafter!"

~&~

"You will marry Alfred Rafter!" Mortimer Warden struck the floor hard with his cane, rebutting Carrie's ongoing argument.

A short man, Carrie's father was the king of his household. With gray hair that now matched his assertive gray eyes, his robust body, although small, impressed his peers with its iron strength. He could be formidable when crossed, and the family seldom chose that option.

Carrie believed she had inherited most of her good traits from her mother. Unfortunately, she had his temper.

"Papa, I do not care for the man!"

"You do not know him well. You must try to ingratiate yourself to win his good graces," he said, obviously controlling his ire. "Also, it is time you made friends with his mother. The house you will be living in is hers until Alfred inherits. They are both waiting to welcome you."

A more dreadful prospect Carrie could not imagine. Condemned to worse than death! She had overheard old Mistress Rafter's opinion of her as well as a retelling of it from her friends.

Mr. Rafter's huge mother loathed the fact that Carrie shunned a more ladylike conveyance to ride horseback. "She should be made to settle down, learn to be a lady," she reportedly declared. As if that were not enough, Mr. Rafter had a nearly grown daughter who also criticized her.

"I am sorry, Papa, but I have no desire to be likable to any of the Rafters. A man of his age and resources should have a dwelling of his own. That aside, I could never marry him even if he had a mansion." Carrie's chin lifted in defiance.

"This is not your decision to make," he said. "Your mother and I have done that for you."

A look at her tiny, slender mother told Carrie her mother had not wholly agreed to the arrangement. Gwendolyn Warden sank slowly into a chair beside the mahogany desk, and her hands trembled as she settled the flounces of her gown. Lowering her head of gray-streaked red hair, she avoided her daughter's scrutiny.

Mortimer's face softened. "Now, Daughter, I do not wish to force you into this alliance. I believe it is merely a matter of directing your mind to what would be the most sensible decision." He walked to the bay window overlooking the drab winter lawn. "We expect Mr. Rafter to have dinner here tonight. You will dress in your best and come down to welcome our guest in a congenial manner."

"Oh, Papa," Carrie protested.

"Carrie! No more conversation. I insist you make the most of this. Hear me now! I will give you a week to make up your mind while you use every day to get better acquainted with Mr. Rafter. This is not a request; it is an order. I'm giving you one week!"

two

At dawn the same morning, Graham Nugent had slid a shiny black boot into the stirrup, swung his leg over the saddle of his black gelding, and settled the reins in his calfskin gloves. Dressed in black riding breeches with a fawn jacket and waistcoat, he touched his riding hat in salute to his parents, watching from their upstairs bedroom window. Resettling himself in the saddle, he jumped Raven over a fence and galloped away as his groom returned to the barn.

The sun had just risen. Raven's hooves raced over the dew-covered field like the flight of the bird that was his namesake. Graham gave him his head, enjoying the speed and the feeling that he was riding the air. Trees rose up before him, spearing the sky with limbs barren of foliage, and he turned the horse to ride through a narrow strip of land leading to the next field. He rode on steadily until he came to a second grove of trees, where he glimpsed a shallow stream shining in the sun. He pulled up and dismounted to give Raven a well-deserved rest and a drink of water.

Minutes later, as he cantered away, Graham relaxed, enjoying his freedom away from the Philadelphia law office where he read law. A partnership had recently been offered him, but he was in no hurry. God had not yet shown him His plan for the future. When the time came, the Lord would make the path clear, and Graham would follow willingly.

His attention was drawn to a lone rider galloping hard. It was a girl, and she seemed lost in the same emotions he enjoyed. In the morning sun, her burnished hair streamed behind her hat like ripples in the stream he had just left. He brought Raven to a halt and simply stared.

The girl seemed bursting with energy, almost more than her tiny body could hold. Surely her ride had generated that exuberance. With her mount in complete control, her bright hair and the trim green riding habit complementing her frame, she became a fantasy, a beautiful vision streaking across the curve of the world.

And then she was gone. Had he only imagined her? No, she was real, flesh and blood. It was the cold morning light that had created that ethereal perception. A real girl had a home and family. She could be found, and his parents could help. He had arrived by coach from Philadelphia last night. Once he was settled in at home for the holidays, he would find out who she was and where he could meet her.

He headed back the way he had come, veering off in the direction of the village at the crossroads. Raven picked up speed, and they loped into the town and down a side street to a modest house with a whitewashed picket fence and a minuscule yard. He stopped at the hitching post and got off, securing Raven's reins and giving him a pat of assurance.

Reverend Thomas answered the door and threw back his head.

"Graham! I had not expected you this morning."

"Is my visit inconvenient? I can come back at a later time if you like."

"Not at all. Please, come in. We'll have Margaret bring us some coffee."

The preacher chuckled as Graham ducked to miss the top of the door when he entered. On the way to the study, the pastor asked his wife to bring coffee, and Graham greeted her with a warm hug.

"It's about time you fit us in for a visit," she said, smiling her pleasure at Graham's presence. "You've been in town a couple of times before without seeing us, but we know how busy you are when you're here."

"I'm ashamed. I'll try to get by more often in the future, I promise." Graham hugged her shoulders again.

"See that you do. Now, go with the pastor, and I'll bring coffee," she said and scurried to the kitchen.

The study they entered reminded Graham of its occupant, formal enough for a man of God but containing a touch of whimsy. Potted geraniums sat on a windowsill above bookshelves lined with Bibles, volumes of Hebrew and Greek, and a stack of homemade notebooks belonging to students Reverend Thomas tutored.

A well-worn desk and an easy chair defined the room. They belonged to a scholar with a need for utter quiet. Yet a picture on one wall held a fanciful view. It depicted a trout fisherman in a rushing stream. A rugged outdoorsman.

Graham hung his hat on the rack and sat in a chair across the desk from the minister. The coffee came, and they traded information about the weather, the village, and Graham's family. The real reason for the visit came at last.

Graham set his cup on the desk. "I had to come, and I hope I'm not keeping you from your work. I always need to talk about my spiritual life when I'm with you."

Reverend Thomas extended his forearms on the desktop and clasped his hands. "Believers have a natural desire to share with one another. It strengthens us in the Lord."

Graham nodded and rubbed his hand across his forehead. "I wonder what the Lord has in store for me. Most of those who read law are interested in nothing else. I long for a friend with whom I can discuss the Bible and pray. In my present situation, I have access to no one like that."

"When I was your age," the reverend said, "I met my Margaret. We were so poor we couldn't afford to get married, but we did anyway. I got from her the support you seem to need now." He smiled broadly. "What about you? Is there a girl out there you feel is special, Graham? Someone you think you might marry?"

"Unfortunately, no." He thought of the girl he had seen riding that morning, but he could not be sure he would even meet her. "Father and Mother would like me to marry. They continually remind me that I'm already twenty-six. They worry that I'll become old and set in my ways like my bachelor uncle, Frederick. He's the one with whom I read law, remember?"

"Oh, yes. I suppose they fear that his unattached status will rub off on you. Am I right?"

Nodding, Graham stood and reached for his hat. The pastor stood too. "I doubt you will remain unmarried. Do you pray for the girl God has for you, Graham? You know that's the first requirement in finding a true mate for life."

Graham's face sobered. "I do indeed, Sir. I know it's God's desire that we marry a believer in Christ, so we will not be unequally yoked. There's no one now, but I'm not discouraged. When the time is right, I believe God will provide that particular lady for me."

The pastor came around his old desk. "Remember what Proverbs 3, verses 5 and 6, have to say, Graham. 'Trust in the Lord with all thine heart; and lean not unto thine own understanding. In all thy ways acknowledge Him, and He shall direct thy paths.' As long as you wait for the Lord's will and timing, Son, you can't go wrong. I predict great things in store for you, including a wonderful wife. It does my heart good to hear that you're on the right track."

They gave each other a bear hug, and the pastor asked if he might pray.

"Thank you, my friend. That's another reason I came."

As they knelt by Graham's chair, the minister asked God's blessing. "Heavenly Father, thank You for this fine visit with Graham. As he develops as a lawyer, he's developing as a Christian, and I'm especially grateful for Your grace in his life. Help him remain strong in the faith, and when it's time, send him the exact girl You've chosen for his wife.

"Bless his family and mine with deeper commitment to You. Make my little congregation yearn to be more like You, Jesus, with love for each other and for the unsaved among us. Give to both Graham and me the strength to do the work You have for us. I pray in Jesus' name. Amen."

When they finished, Reverend Thomas walked Graham to the door.

"Did you invite him to the Christmas Eve program, Dear?" Margaret asked.

"I did, and he promised to come."

"Wonderful! We'll look forward to seeing you and your family then, Graham. You come back and see us."

She kissed his cheek, and the pastor opened the door and shook his hand as Graham walked out into the cool day.

At the gate, a small boy stood beside Raven, the reins of a butternut pony held loosely in his hand. Petting Raven's neck, he whispered to him, and Raven nickered a soft answer. Graham had never seen the horse respond to a stranger that way before. Astonished, he sauntered toward the boy.

"You like horses, do you?" he asked, smiling at the child.

"I like this beauty. Is he yours, Sir?" Enthusiasm lit the boy's face.

"He is indeed, and he seems to like you." Graham put out a hand and stroked the nose of the pony. "You have a nice mount too. What do you call him?"

"Bandy."

"My name is Graham Nugent, and who are you?"

"Trouble—uh, I mean, Travis Warden, Sir."

Graham laughed out loud. "I suspect you don't appreciate your pet name, Travis."

"I don't mind too much, Sir. The truth is, I do get into trouble at times, in fact more times than not. But I do it mostly by mistake."

Trying not to laugh at the boy's serious defense, Graham moved to Raven's side, stepped up into the saddle, and smiled down at the boy.

"What do you say we continue this conversation as we ride? I need to get back home, west of the settlement. Are you going in that direction?"

"No, I go in the opposite direction, but Bandy and I ride all over. We can ride along with you for awhile."

Trouble mounted his butternut pony and turned him to draw abreast of Raven. The boy and the man rode off together at a comfortable trot. They had ridden silently for only a short time when Bandy tripped over a tree root and bounced Trouble free of his hat.

"Ho, Bandy! I lost my hat!" He tumbled off the pony

and dashed behind Bandy to grab a tan wool knitted cap with a strange brim. He jammed it carelessly on his head of curly red hair and ran back.

"That's quite a hat," Graham said, thinking about the mass of red-gold hair he had admired earlier that day.

"It's a sorry hat. Sorry," Trouble stated grimly. "I wouldn't wear it, but Carrie knitted it so my ears would stay warm. Now I have to wear it." He sighed. "She did her best."

Graham smothered a laugh while Trouble got back on his pony. He enjoyed the boy's humor tremendously. They started off, and Graham posed another question.

"Who is this Carrie? A little lady friend of yours?"

Trouble's face twisted with chagrin. "Naw! Carrie is my older sister. She can cook good, and she can do things good around the house. But she's just no good at sewing and knitting and such as that. A pure failure."

While Graham's first response favored laughter, his heart pounded with a rapid thud. Was it possible that Travis's older sister, Carrie, was the vision he had seen riding this morning?

"Why don't we find out a bit about each other, Travis? You tell me something about your family, and I'll do the same. Take riding, for instance. Do any other members of your family ride?"

"Well, my papa's name is Mortimer Warden. Mama's name is Gwendolyn. Neither of them rides. My brothers Caleb and Joshua do, and they work for Papa at the mills."

Trouble guided Bandy around a village well, where

two women were drawing up a bucket of water to fill a tub. Graham stopped. He dismounted, drew the water, emptied a bucketful into the small tub, and drew another. Giggling, the women thanked him and, with the tub between them, marched arduously down the pathway leading to a neighborhood of small cottages.

On their way again, Trouble addressed Graham seriously. "You were very polite. You were a hero to those women, I think. They thought you were pretty."

Graham again laughed out loud. "Pretty? Men are not pretty, Travis. They are handsome. But, tell me, how would you know if those women thought me pretty?"

The look of boredom on Trouble's face gave away his sentiments on the subject. "Because I've seen the same look on the faces of men who try to court my sister, Carrie. They get silly expressions, and they act foolish."

Graham's emotions were doing somersaults. He didn't know this girl, but he did not like the idea of other men dancing attendance on his fantasy. Yet, wasn't he being presumptuous? The girl might not even be the one he had seen riding. He still hadn't found out.

"So, you four are your parents' only offspring?"

"No, besides Carrie, there's one more girl, Virgie. She's married. So are my brothers. Carrie and I are the only ones who live at home." He wound the pony's reins around his hands. "Why don't we gallop for awhile? I'm getting tired of crawling along. Doesn't Raven like a good run?"

"Of course, but would you answer this before we go?

Just by accident I saw a girl out riding this morning. Is Carrie's hair the same color as yours?"

"Red, you mean? Yes, only mine's darker. Hers looks like sunshine. Carrie's my best friend. I like her even better than my brothers. She's never too busy to be with me, and she listens when I want to talk. Not everyone can get along with her, though. She can get real furious at times. She and Papa are mixed up in a feud right now." He lifted Bandy's reins. "Ready? Set? Go!"

Trouble kicked the butternut pony, and the animal took off as if he had been released from a hobble. Graham hesitated, wishing the boy had finished the story; but he had to keep up, or he might not find out anything. He set Raven at a gallop through the sparse trees until he rode within a few yards of the boy.

Overgrown grass and dead leaves softened the horses' hoofbeats as they raced over the cold sod, the man making sure the boy won the race. Graham could smell the moist air of the nearby river. It was invigorating. The sun was full out now, making the day perfect for such an outing.

Trouble's urge for speed ran out, and the two walked their horses, giving Graham another chance to question him. At first he made jokes and talked of hunting and trapping, subjects that interested the boy. Then he returned the conversation to Trouble's sister.

"It may have been your sister I saw riding this morning. It was just after dawn. Is Carrie an early riser?"

"Most of the time. Unless she reads a book late or is invited to a party the night before. But I think she did ride early this morning. Mr. Rafter came, and she got out of the house so she wouldn't have to see him. Papa was angry as I've ever seen him. That's what started the quarrel."

"Who is Mr. Rafter?"

"He's the man Papa wants Carrie to marry. She says she won't, but he says she will. I don't blame her. Mr. Rafter is too old." Trouble gave Graham a man-to-man look. "Usually, though, Papa gets his way." He craned his neck to look up toward the sun. "Uh-oh, I'll miss my lunch if I don't hurry. I'll tell Papa about our ride, and maybe he'll invite you to visit us soon."

Graham held out his hand for a good-bye, and Trouble gave it a manly shake. They smiled, each turning a different way. Graham urged Raven to a canter while putting together what he had learned.

His fantasy was no fantasy. Carrie did exist, and she was the sister of Travis Warden, his small companion. Her father had apparently arranged a marriage with a man she did not care for. He wondered just how old this man Rafter was. For that matter, how old was Carrie? Too young to claim his interest? From his short glimpse of her, he did not think so. He would fill in the blanks as soon as possible and proceed from there.

Why did he have this yearning to know more about her? Was it the latest suggestion that it was time for him to marry? Maybe. Or could it be God, once again directing his path? He smiled in excitement at the possibility.

Kicking Raven into a gallop, he soon recognized the family property and decided he felt ready for lunch too.

three

The evening with Alfred Rafter turned into the worst hours of Carrie's life. Returning from an errand in the kitchen, she thought of her grim future and mentally cast about for an escape from the evening and from the village.

The shallow conversation she'd been forced to endure all evening filtered from the parlor. To Carrie it resembled the chatter of schoolchildren, not adults. Closing her ears to the sound, she recalled the bitter quarrel with her father about Alfred Rafter that very afternoon.

Mortimer Warden, owner of Warden Mills, was an intimidating opponent. Though gentle on rare occasions, he was known to argue another businessman into utter silence with his strength of will and articulate speech. Most particularly, his temper rose to the danger level when his obstinate daughter opposed him.

Carrie's mistake that day was picking the wrong time to speak to him. He resented her intrusion into his office during an already frustrating day.

"Say what you came to say, Carrie, then please take yourself out of here. I have my accounts to go over again. Incompetent employees! This family doesn't appreciate what I go through. None of you knows how hard I work to keep a roof over your heads, to say nothing of your food, clothing, and the extras you require. What is it you want now?"

Carrie, accustomed to his paranoid attacks, was prepared. She answered calmly, "Papa, I know how good you are to us. All I have to do is look at this beautiful house and its expensive furniture to know what a good businessman you are."

"Hmm, about time you noticed." Her father went back to his accounts, brow furrowed and his attention to her replaced by pages of numerals.

Carrie plunged ahead. "Papa, if you'd let me, I believe I could help with your business."

Pen in midair, Mortimer looked up, his eyes wide. "You? How could you help?"

She sat on the edge of the chair near his desk. "Well, Papa, I told you Alice Garner has invited me to visit her in New York, and you know how much I'd like to go. But what you may not know is that her father is very well acquainted there. He runs a large mercantile business. I was thinking that while I'm there I could tell him about my clever father in Maryland, with mills on the Chesapeake, and how smart it would be to set up trade with you."

Her father had exploded out of his chair. "What? Carrie! I won't allow you to even think such a thing! I handle the business in this family. Do you think we would allow you to travel to New York alone, to visit who knows who? I'm ashamed of you! You concentrate on marrying Alfred Rafter. That's the way to increase my business, and that is all that's required of you."

It took a lengthy verbal assault aimed at her character to finally satisfy his fury and settle him back into his chair with his accounts. Carrie slunk out of the room, defeated. But she had not given up. She couldn't give up.

When Rafter arrived that evening, he brought his large, odious daughter, Ermagene, too. The man seemed to think she was the magic charm that would win Carrie's affection. Oddly, and for the first time, her parents seemed to falter in their approval of the man with whom they had made the arrangement.

"Mistress Warden, may I offer our felicitations on the delicious repast you presented at table? Delightful fare, was it not, Ermagene?" The dandified suitor dipped into his snuff.

"An ample sufficiency," Ermagene answered with a saucy tone.

Gwendolyn spoke from her seat on the couch beside her husband. "I must pass on the compliment to my cook. She has been with us for years, and we think she's quite remarkable."

Unable to delay her entrance any longer, Carrie moved forward. She set a bowl of fruit and a plate of sweet-meats and taffy on a table near their guests.

They had retired to the big living room after dinner. A huge sandstone fireplace with a green tapestry screen dominated one end of the room. At the opposite end sat a tall Christmas tree. Partially decorated, it would attain its full grandeur at their Christmas Eve party when colorful presents and myriad candles were added.

Carrie left the refreshment table and took a seat on a stool covered with a peculiar needlepoint only she could have stitched. Her hope to remain unnoticed evaporated when Alfred Rafter and Ermagene immediately engaged her in conversation.

Rafter claimed attention first. "Now, Miss Warden, I must say I'm disappointed. You have been reluctant to enter into our conversation this evening. Are you feeling unwell?"

"No, I am very well," she said tersely.

Ermagene examined Carrie's features. "Considering your circumstances, I expected you to welcome us with more enthusiasm. My dear mama was a wonderful hostess. She taught me always to be gracious to our guests."

Carrie smiled sweetly. "Then I would say you were fortunate to have such a mother. If I were you, I would do anything to keep my father from replacing her."

Conversation stopped abruptly. Mortimer stared at Carrie, incredulous. Jumping up to inspect the plate of candy, Trouble overturned his stool with a crash.

Gwendolyn, obviously grateful for the interruption, addressed her son. "Travis, Dear, you have had all the sweets you need tonight. It's late and far past your bedtime. Take your candle from the hall and light your way upstairs."

"Oh, Mama."

"Trouble—" Agitated, Gwendolyn rose.

"Oh, all right," the boy muttered. He turned to his father and gave him a kiss, then back to his mother and kissed her. "Good night, Mr. Rafter and Miss Rafter." With a little bow, he turned away. Sneaking as close to Carrie as he dared, he murmured, "Don't give in."

Slightly embarrassed, Gwendolyn apologized. "I'm sorry for the need to discipline in front of company—"

Rafter held up a hand to counter her intention and shook his head with closed eyes. "I thought you used extraordinary restraint, Ma'am. Had it been mine to administer, he would have had a good slap to remind him not to answer back."

Even Mortimer tightened his mouth to prevent a quick reply. Carrie was offended too. Trouble was adventurous but not sassy. In a moment Mortimer was able to offer a meager smile and switch to a subject related to Rafter's business. The women listened silently until the boring hour spent itself.

The evening ended with no less tension, and Carrie felt her father grateful when the Rafters left. She expected a lecture from him afterward, but none occurred. He indicated only that they would talk later, and he went to bed. Evidently the stress of the evening had left him too exhausted to deal with more dialogue.

In her room, Carrie found her brother cuddled on her bed in his nightshirt.

"Trouble, what are you doing here?" she whispered.

Half awake, he mumbled, "Are you going out riding early in the morning?"

"Of course, Dear. I always do."

"Good." He dragged himself off the bed and mean-dered sleepily to the door.

❧

Trouble slipped out before dawn the next morning. The darkness made it difficult to saddle Bandy, but he managed without waking any of the servants. He had learned the location of the Nugent home and headed in that direction.

It took longer than he had planned to get to Graham's house because Bandy's caution in the murky light slowed them. Trouble hadn't counted on all those ghostly shadows.

Few people in the village were up this early. The light of the waning moon soon dissolved in the cold air. Trouble wondered if either of the riders he wanted to bring together would venture out on such a frosty morning. Grateful for Carrie's misshapen wool hat, he had also worn extra clothing against the cold beneath his heavy sack coat.

On the last lap of his shadowy trip, he picked out the house, then the barn he was looking for. There were no house lights. Quiet hung over the land. He stopped on a mound near the house. Slipping from the saddle, he found a seat on the trunk of a fallen tree and prepared to wait.

No more than ten minutes passed, Trouble thought, before someone left the back door and walked to the barn. The eastern sky had turned lighter now, and he could identify Graham Nugent. He got on Bandy and rode down toward him.

Under a black greatcoat, Graham wore the same fawn

jacket Trouble had seen him in before. Alert, he stopped to await the approaching rider.

"Who—? Travis, is that you?"

"Yes, Sir."

Graham laid his hand on the boy's arm. "What are you doing here? Is everything all right?"

"Yes, Sir, I'm fine. I came to ride with you if you'll let me. If you intend to go." Trouble's courage fled in the face of the man's hesitance.

Graham chuckled. "If you got up this early to ride with me, how can I refuse? Would you like to help me saddle up?"

The boy slid off his pony and joined him.

❧

Thoughts tumbled in Graham's mind. Again he wondered, *Is this God's leading?* Would he meet his fantasy today, and would she be the one? He led the way inside, and Travis tied Bandy at the door. Raven nickered, ready to go at the sight of his master. With the boy's help, the gelding was saddled in minutes.

They rode out of the barn lot and down the hill, Graham wondering if Travis would disclose further secrets about his family without prompting. No sooner had they lost sight of the house than Travis opened up.

"Mr. Nugent, you should have been at our house last night. Old Mr. Rafter and his daughter came to dinner."

Remembering the look Travis gave him as he broke the news that "Papa" wanted Carrie to marry Mr. Rafter, Graham offered a word of caution. "Are you sure your sister would approve of this man-to-man conversation?"

Bobbing along on Bandy, Travis put on a startled face. "You wouldn't tell Carrie, would you?"

"No. When gentlemen talk to others, they do not speak of their private conversations." Graham wanted to laugh, but he didn't dare. "What you tell me will go no further."

"Then would you like to hear what happened?"

"If you want to tell me, Travis."

"Carrie was supposed to be extra nice to Mr. Rafter and his daughter, Ermagene, but at dinner she kept her head down and didn't speak unless someone asked her a question. The daughter talked mean to her until she finally made Carrie mad, and Carrie said something that made Papa's face turn red."

Graham wasn't sure he wanted to hear those details. "I'm sorry that happened, Travis. I hope Carrie can forget her words and forgive her."

Travis was too swept up by the memory to stop. "Mama sent me to bed, so I don't know what happened after that. But I told Carrie if Papa tries to make her marry Mr. Rafter, she should run away, and I would help her."

Graham felt guilty he had allowed Travis to confide in him. They slowed to a walk, and he decided he should send the boy home and ride on alone. He halted Raven.

"Travis, I think it's a mistake for you to talk about a subject that is this private to your sister. Perhaps you should go home now. No doubt your breakfast is waiting, and I'm sure you don't want to miss it."

"No!" said Travis. "You mustn't leave! We won't see—"

Graham rose in his stirrups. "Who is that?" He pointed to a figure galloping toward them on horseback.

His heart suddenly beat faster. It was the same girl he had seen the day before.

"I think it's my sister." Travis smiled in excitement. "It is! It's Carrie!" He lifted an eager face. "I'd like to introduce you. Do you want to meet her? I'm sure you'd like her."

Graham was beginning to understand. "Why, yes, certainly. I would like very much to meet your sister," he said, grinning.

He looked down at his clothes and brushed at his breeches. If he had known, he would have worn better riding apparel. It made no difference; he had to meet Carrie. Then God would either lead him away or draw them closer.

The girl saw them and slowed her mare to a canter. Travis trotted Bandy out to meet her. Her eyes examined Graham intently as she advanced.

Their introduction burst breathlessly from Travis. "This is my sister, Sir. Carrie, this is my friend, Mr. Nugent." He backed his pony to prompt the other two to talk.

"Graham Nugent, Miss Warden. I am very glad to meet you. Travis has spoken of you at length."

Carrie Warden blushed and seemed at a loss for words. Framed by golden red hair, her countenance was so lovely, Graham thought his heart would pound out of his chest.

Below a tiny upturned nose, her slightly raised chin

spoke of an independent spirit. A slender neck, high cheekbones, and an ivory complexion elegantly accompanied the most beautiful mouth he had ever seen. Graham found he couldn't take his eyes off it.

Carrie murmured a polite greeting and turned her horse to direct a stare at Travis. "May I ask what you are up to this morning? I assumed you had a reason when you asked me if I were going out early to ride." Her eyes held a suspicious look.

"I, uh. . .just wondered because I was going too," he rambled, his expression a little sheepish.

"Then why did you not wait for me? When you didn't come to my door, I looked into your room, and you were already gone."

Disconcerted, Graham realized Travis was being reprimanded for doing him a favor. He gave Raven a gentle heel opposite Carrie's view, and the big horse sidestepped.

"Whoa, Boy, whoa," he murmured, patting Raven's neck. "Beg pardon, I didn't mean to interrupt. But since we're here, and we all seem to be dressed for it, might we continue riding the meadows as we talk?"

"That would be telling my brother that whatever he decides to do on his own is permissible. What if Mother had looked for him and found him gone? She would have been beside herself with worry. As it is, she knows he's with me. I left a note."

Graham smiled, satisfied. "So then everything's all right." He tightened Raven's reins. "Excellent! Away we go!"

A frown creased Carrie's face, and he knew he had made

a mistake. She did not appreciate being ordered about in such a high-handed manner. Before he could apologize, she turned on him.

"Everything is not all right! Trouble, we're leaving."

Travis looked so forlorn Graham tried to rectify his action. "Wait! Let me explain." He smoothed one glove with the other. "I believe. . .I think Travis just wanted to do something. . .nice for someone."

She turned to Travis. "What, Trouble? What is he talking about?"

Travis shrugged innocently. "I, I just. . ."

Holding her riding crop, Carrie made a fist and placed it on her hip. "This is ridiculous! Someone tell me the truth! What are you two talking about?"

"Miss Warden, I'm afraid this cannot be explained. I made a promise to Travis, and I can't break it."

"Travis! You mean Trouble! We call him that because trouble is his principal occupation." She touched her brother lightly in the chest with her whip. "Now, tell me the truth, Trouble. Why did you meet with Mr. Nugent, and what nice thing did you do for him that he can't disclose?"

"I can't tell you."

"Yes, you certainly can. I insist!"

Graham could no longer remain silent. "Travis, what you did is not so bad. If I understand your motive, you were only trying to do a favor, am I correct?"

Travis's head lowered. He evidently found it hard to face his sister. Finally he muttered, "I'm trying to get you out of marrying old Mr. Rafter. I thought if you met and liked each other, maybe you could marry Mr. Nugent."

Her countenance crimson, Carrie pressed gloved hands to her face to cover her mortification. "Trouble!" she gasped. "Trouble, how could you? Have you no shame?"

"Please, Miss Warden. Don't blame your brother," Graham said. "He loves you very much." Startled by her look of resentment, he added softly, "He meant to help you."

"Is that what you thought you were doing, Trouble?" she asked, her expression still stern.

"Yes! I met Mr. Nugent, and I liked him. I thought if I could get him for you, you wouldn't have to marry that old man."

Graham held his breath. If Travis could have irritated his sister more, Graham could not imagine how. Carrie's pallor almost frightened him.

Her body stiffened. Ignoring him, she addressed her brother. "I will see you at home, young man," she said quietly.

For Graham, her stare was deadly. "As for you, Mr. Nugent, it is my sincere desire that I never see you again as long as I live!" With a light stroke of her whip, she turned the mare and galloped away.

Graham looked at the little boy. Travis had the saddest face he had ever seen. "Don't be downhearted, my young friend. I promise you this is not the end. It is only the beginning."

four

Tears coursing down her cheeks, Carrie rode furiously over the rolling fields and away from Graham Nugent. She wished with all her heart she were far away where no one could see her. How could her brother betray her so? How could he deliberately tell that man about her problem and confess that he actually thought she might marry Mr. Nugent?

Trouble had disgraced her, humiliated her! Graham Nugent would laugh every time he thought about the incident. Then he'd tell his friends, and they would laugh. He would share every nuance of the joke with them. Never could she show her face in public again. And confront Graham Nugent? Impossible! She was trapped at home forever.

If only Trouble would come home soon and not stay with the man. There must be straight talk between them, with Mama as the arbiter. It made no difference that the ugly subject of the arrangement might rear up again. So be it. But could Mama possibly understand her situation?

Frantic, she swiped at her tears. Maybe it wouldn't be so bad. It might turn out well. She could apprise her mother of the dilemma with Graham Nugent and, in a roundabout way, inform her that Papa's edict had placed her in that position. Mama might even persuade Papa to call the whole thing off. *Oh, if only he would.*

Her tiny green hat with its single golden feather flew off in the direction she had come, but she did not care. She wanted only to get back to the safety of her home. The hat and her riding habit were old. She should have had a complete new ensemble long ago.

The reason she didn't surfaced, and she frowned. Papa forced her to wear the old green suit. Convinced she rode her horse to excess, he decided her favorite activity was immodest, and he did not want her riding out so much. She suspected the Rafters also disapproved of this practice, and naturally their opinions became Papa's.

Sensing her rider's lack of concentration, the mare slowed. Though Carrie tried to forget the Rafters, her mind disobeyed. What if she found herself facing the actual wedding day with Alfred Rafter? No. Such a thing simply couldn't happen. Yet what else could she do? As Trouble said, she could run away. But run away to where?

She knew little of the world's realities. She had lived at home, gone to Miss Stimson's School for Young Ladies for two years, then lived back at home again. She lived within the confines of her family. At this moment, though, home was the location she most desired.

As she crossed the brook below their property, her skirt sagged into the water, doing more damage and causing the costume to look even shabbier. Graham Nugent must have noticed its downtrodden state. If she met him out riding again after this. . . But she would not! She mustn't ever talk to him again. She didn't dare.

Why did he have to be so attractive? Honesty presented itself, and she couldn't deny her feelings. She saw herself in a prison, and through the bars she could see a delightful open park, full of flowers. She caught her breath. That exact feeling encompassed her when she looked at Graham Nugent.

His coal black hair waved and curled above his collar just the way it should to set off his intelligent face with its firm jaw and deep blue eyes. His eyes spoke for him at times, and she wondered if he knew it. He sat his horse as if born to ride, his broad shoulders square and straight. His riding apparel fit as if his flesh had been melted down and poured into the tasteful selection.

Now she might never see him again; her brother had seen to that. But despite being angry with Trouble, she couldn't fault him. He had wanted only her good. He knew she hated the idea of an arranged marriage, and he had tried to help. Papa was at fault.

Fathers were supposed to do their best for their unmarried daughters. Yet did they? Neither Virgie nor she had been given a choice. Maybe wealthy girls of marriageable age would someday be permitted to choose their own spouses. No, such an idea bordered on the absurd. The supremacy of male knowledge and choices would always prevail. Tears rose in Carrie's eyes again. What a dismal future. For the lowly female, there was no hope of escape.

She'd thought of other possibilities, but nothing had worked. There was little chance of continuing her education. She'd mentioned a tutor to Papa, and he had ordered her out of the room.

Remembering her desire to travel, she grimaced. For two years she had begged to go to New York to visit Alice Garner, but Papa would not hear of it. Her conversation about the girl's father helping Papa's business prospects had brought him almost to the limit of his hot temper, so that was a closed issue too.

Before she moved, Alice and Carrie were close friends. It was the longest friendship Papa had ever allowed, and there was a specific reason. Alice and her family did not attend church. Papa had assumed that, as a member of the Garner family, Alice would not oppose her father's philosophy, his negative opinion of the church. And Mortimer Warden would not have his daughter stray.

In looks and temperament, Alice was the opposite of Carrie. Her unexceptional dark hair and gray eyes deceived many people as to her worth. But not Carrie. She grew to idolize Alice, who personified everything she wanted to be.

When she was nine, it had taken only minutes at a property sale Papa and the family attended to become attached to Alice. Oddly, they liked each other with the first glance.

At the back of the house to be sold, Carrie saw Alice, her patchwork skirt flying high, pumping a rope swing into the air.

"Well, what are you gawking at?" the older girl called. "I bet you've never even been on a swing, have you? You're too nice! You'd dirty up that lacy pink dress of yours."

"I wouldn't mind," Carrie said, wishing the girl would invite her to try the swing regardless of certain punishment from her parents.

"Maybe you wouldn't, but I'll bet that snooty pa of yours would. Probably fall over dead with a stopped heart." The girl smiled mischievously. "Wanna try?"

Carrie had tried, and she never forgot the thrill of the experience. They became friends. Alice's spirit called out a spark of rebellion in Carrie that never left.

But that was long ago. When Carrie turned fourteen, her friend moved away, and it had taken Carrie months to get over the loss. Through the years Alice had listened to her troubles with Papa and encouraged Carrie to be true to herself. A few letters found their way back and forth, yet it was only when Trouble grew older and he and Carrie became closer, that Carrie's need for true companionship was satisfied.

Wishing she could share her present problem with Alice, Carrie whipped Samantha into a gallop, jumped the mare over a low hedge, and raced on toward the Warden property. Thoughts of her childhood friend encouraged her to approach her mother, and beyond the house she slowed the mare to a walk and guided her into the barn.

*

In her sitting room, Carrie's mother sat holding a lace-edged pillowcase, her dainty fingers sending a flashing needle in and out of an embroidery pattern. Papa required Carrie to let her mother know when she came back from her ride, but she intended to make short work of this appearance. Her face and nose were swollen from crying, and she didn't want her mother to start asking questions.

"I'm glad you're home, Dear," Gwendolyn said, too absorbed in her work to look up. "I'd like to talk to you about our Christmas celebration. I have the food list here from last year." She laid down her work and handed Carrie a slip of paper. "Have you any changes or additions to suggest?"

Swollen face or not, Carrie saw the quiet of the room as an opportunity to discuss the terrible night before, and she snatched at it. "Mama, didn't last night show you how badly matched Alfred Rafter and I are? Please try to understand. I could never be happy in that home. Won't you try to see the situation from my side?"

Her mother still did not look up. Carrie noticed a slight tremble in her hands as she drew the thread through the fabric on her lap. "The situation has been arranged, and you are to settle the matter in your mind in one week," Gwendolyn said, reciting her husband's warning. "You will be well taken care of. Instead of opposing it, you should be thinking of the advantages of the marriage!"

Crying, Carrie went down on her knees before her mother. "Oh, Mama, can't you feel what it's like to be me? How can I marry a man old enough to be my father? He has a mother and a daughter who hate me.

Not only have I overheard his mother's negative comments, but others I trust have divulged her complaints about me."

Gwendolyn smoothed the hair of Carrie's bowed head and raised her chin to look at her. "Carrie, Dear, there is nothing I can do. Your father has decided, and you know he's. . . Your father is always right in these matters."

"Oh, Mama, that's the problem. You think Papa is always right, and Papa is under the Rafters' control. Do you think he has thought seriously about my future? Put yourself in my place, Mama. Tell me the truth. Do you honestly want to see me married for the rest of my life to a man I don't love?"

Her mother twisted in her chair. "You're not looking at the facts, Carrie. You must realize there are certain adjustments every couple has to make in order to find happiness in marriage. Even your father and I had to make adjustments." Her voice faltered as if she were uncertain she'd made a valid point.

"But, Mama—"

"No more, Carrie! Please, leave me be!" Her mother grabbed her embroidery, tried twice to stuff it into her sewing basket, and with a sob clasped it in her arms and hurried from the room.

Shocked, Carrie remembered the earlier scene with Virgie. But Virgie's case was different. When her sister stomped from the room, her needlework in hand, Carrie felt relief just to have the harassment end. In the current situation, she felt guilty she had caused her mother such despair and brought her to tears.

Warily rising to her feet, Carrie left the room, her emotions in turmoil. Two problems existed. On the one hand, her temper had erased the possibility of seeing Graham Nugent again. Even if she wanted to, there was no honorable way to approach him. On the other hand, the arranged marriage to Alfred Rafter would put an end to her life. Was there no way out? Nothing to look forward to? She had to face facts; she would never be happy again.

&

Graham had a plan. He and his parents would attend the Christmas program at their church, where Reverend Thomas was pastor; but that evening, after the program, the festivities could be extended. Seated at their dining room table for the evening meal, Riley Nugent, Graham's father, offered prayer.

"Heavenly Father, we praise Your name for sending us Your Son, the Light of life. As we come again to the season when we celebrate His birth, we're especially conscious of the many blessings You have bestowed on us, and we thank You. Having Graham home from the law office is a special blessing. In gratitude, we give of ourselves as You gave the example. Thank You for this food, our salvation, and the Word we have hidden in our hearts. In Jesus' name. Amen."

Hearing his father pray again comforted Graham. Being home with his parents filled a need like nothing else. He loved his childhood home.

Decorated in the pastels his mother favored, the house featured large rooms full of light. The cherry and walnut furniture had been crafted by the Riley Nugent Company. What started as a woodshop was now a thriving business employing a dozen workers.

Graham was proud of his mother and father. For the first time, he noticed they were beginning to show their age. But they were still joyful servants of the Lord, and their hearts and minds remained young. Their gray hair matched, though his father's roundness contrasted sharply with the slender form of his mother, whom he had never seen sitting idle.

He thought again of Carrie Warden. Was she the one God meant him to share a home with? Whether she was or not, he hoped the Lord would send that special girl soon. He wanted to bless his parents with grandchildren, for they had much to teach young ones about the Lord.

The three Nugents dined on a feast of roast pork trimmed with sugared crabapples, vinegar-preserved lima beans, and long potato slices, buttered and baked. Biscuits, nearly light enough to float off the plate, accompanied the meal, and a housemaid waited to serve pudding covered with sweetened cream for dessert.

Halfway through their meal, Graham proposed his plan. "Father, Mother, I have a request. Why don't we have a Christmas party here after the program at church on Christmas Eve?" He waited, sure of their reaction.

Mary Nugent smiled at her husband as she answered. "We were talking about having a party only last night.

There are some new people in our church, and we thought with your being home, it might be the perfect time for a welcome party."

Not exactly what he had in mind. Glancing at the two, Graham suggested, "We could also issue invitations to some of the country people we don't know too well."

"And who might that be?" Riley asked with a raised eyebrow, suspecting his son's real motivation.

"What about the Mortimer Wardens and their children?"

His parents exchanged expressions, and their glance warned Graham that they were reluctant to speak. He hadn't expected this.

They waited for him to comment further.

"Uh, I haven't met the parents," he said. "But I have met young Travis, and he introduced me to his sister Carrie. They're a charming pair."

He was right; he had been duped. He watched his father's grin graduate to a chuckle as he laid his fork aside. Graham waited for the onslaught.

"Charming, eh? Yes, Trouble's freckles are charming. But what could you possibly find charming about the girl?" Riley asked, still smiling.

Graham faced the question soberly. "She's not just any girl, Father. I hope you two will help me. She's angry with me right now because of a mistake Trouble made. I've called him Travis up to now, but I'm beginning to believe the nickname Trouble fits his personality far better. Today he thoroughly embarrassed his sister. I was caught between lying and keeping my word, so I did nothing until she finally galloped away on that little mare of hers."

Mary Nugent's dark eyes probed his. "Your voice tells me you are almost distraught by this. Why?" A maid entered from the kitchen, and Mary signaled her to clear the table.

When the girl left, Graham answered, "I may as well confess. I'm fascinated by her. She's small, pretty, delicate, intelligent—"

"Oh, Graham, Dear." Mary closed her eyes momentarily, and her son searched the serious faces of both his parents.

"What is it? Why are you disturbed?" he asked, not actually wanting the answers.

Riley sipped his water and, leaning back in his chair, rotated the goblet in front of him. "Graham, you are our only child, and you had a few, uh. . .restless years after you became a Christian; but our main desire, for you to follow the Lord, was granted.

"As you began to grow deeper and deeper in Christ, we foresaw nothing to deter your growth. You are a son to be proud of, and more than anything we'd like to see you settled in a home with a fine Christian girl who loves the Lord as much as you."

Clearing his throat, he adjusted small spectacles on his broad nose. "Yes, I'm getting to a point. The facts are these: The Wardens are not members of our church, nor are they members of any church. They're not believers, Graham."

Graham waited for more, but his father and mother were silent. "You mean they are not believers to your knowledge. Many people live their Christian lives without testifying vocally about their faith. Isn't it possible they fall in that category?"

"It isn't just that, Graham. The Wardens are adamant in their opposition to our beliefs. At least, Mortimer is adamant, and in that family his opinion is the only one that counts. He's bitter because, unfortunately, a long time ago an innocent woman in his family was put out of the church," he continued. "Not even their married children attend church, though I know people who belong to other congregations have asked them again and again."

Details pieced themselves together in Graham's mind. Mortimer Warden's word was law. The fact that Carrie must wed Alfred Rafter amounted to a command she dared not refuse. Evidently no compromise existed. Small wonder Trouble became desperate. He loved his sister, and what his father had done to Carrie amounted to betrayal.

Much as he wanted to hurtle the obstacles to become friends with Carrie, and possibly more, the fact that she was not a believer stunned him. The Lord made it clear in His Word that believers should not willfully marry unbelievers. Differences between men and women could be overcome in the Lord, but without Him estrangements lay only a word away. This was certainly a setback.

He took a bite of dessert and waited for the shock to

lessen. His parents ate in silence for several minutes, then Mary placed her spoon on her dessert plate and let her hands drop to her lap.

"I find myself caught between wanting what you desire and wanting what's best. God didn't promise Christians would never be disappointed. His Word asks us to be obedient. Obedience, for the Christian, means having the best things in life according to God's will, and His will is far more satisfying than our own frivolous desires."

Graham remained silent. His mother was right. If Carrie did not believe that Jesus died for her sins, she was not the girl for him. Still, weren't Christians supposed to reach out to those who didn't know the Savior? What if the Wardens came to the party, found the fellowship edifying, and wished to know its source? There might be a chance. . . .

As if he had read Graham's mind, his father spoke again. "Perhaps we should invite the Wardens to the program at the church. If they won't consent to come to the program, it may be they'll come to our party."

"And this very night we'll start praying that the Holy Spirit will begin His work in their hearts," Mary added brightly.

five

The Nugent invitation arrived the next day by messenger. Mortimer, already returned from his daily trip to the mills, was in his office. Aware that a letter had been delivered for her father, Carrie watched as the maid took it to him. He grabbed the letter off the tray and excused the girl brusquely.

Hidden from view by a basket of indigo-dyed cattails in the hall, Carrie winced at the rude dismissal. It reminded her how Papa had, in an underhanded manner, hired the maid away from a competitor's home near Chesapeake Bay. Papa had no scruples when it came to business. That was the category she fitted into. Her life was business as far as he was concerned.

Spying Carrie moving slowly toward him, Mortimer raised a gray eyebrow at her interest and slashed the envelope with a brass letter opener. Carrie sat quietly in a corner chair as her father read the letter, but he did not read it aloud as she would have liked. She watched his face. It took only seconds to comprehend his mood. She felt sorry for the writer; that unlucky businessman would remember this day well.

"Church!" Mortimer's face turned a familiar shade of red. "A party honoring new members of their oh-so-holy

religious congregation and—their son! Read this thing!"
He thrust the missive at her and threw the envelope to
the floor.

Carrie took the costly parchment note and began reading aloud:

> *The Riley Nugents invite their friends to a delightful*
> *evening. We would be honored if you would attend our*
> *Christmas program at the Community Church, after*
> *which our celebration will culminate with a party at*
> *our home. Our son, Graham, is with us for the holidays,*
> *and we joyfully look forward to Christmas Eve with*
> *your lovely family and ours.*

Although signed with the names of Mr. and Mistress
Nugent, the stroke was definitely masculine. Carrie's
face flushed with warmth as she ruminated on just who
might have penned the missive. Her father's probing
look made it impossible to escape the room without a
comment. He expected a question at least, but she was
bereft of sound.

Seconds ticked by. Posing the most benign question
she could think of, she asked, "What shall we reply,
Papa? I'll be glad to write it for you. If we hurry, I might
still be able to catch the messenger."

Mortimer Warden's face lost none of its color. "Reply?
You think trash of this sort deserves a reply?" His fist
pounded the desk, and he spat words Carrie had never
heard before. Finally, without excusing himself, he

stopped, smoothed his leather jerkin, and pulled himself together.

"You may write a simple note, refusing the invitation, and that is all. Write it, and I would like to see the note before it is sent. I'm sure you know my reasons."

He pulled an account book from his desk drawer and slammed it on the desk. Carrie took it for granted she had been dismissed. She stole quietly from the room and headed for her mother's sitting room to accomplish the chore assigned her.

Naturally her father asked to see her reply to the note. He didn't trust her to communicate with the outside world without his say-so. Virgie had stayed close to home until a suitable husband could be found for her. Carrie was the problem child who defied Papa on almost every serious issue. She was entitled to no consideration.

She arrived at her mother's sitting room in such a dismal mood that the brightness of the light-filled room startled her. Her mother sat reading beneath a window hung with a pink half curtain.

Carrie pulled out the chair to the secretary and lowered the writing shelf. As she seated herself, she said, "I have a task to discharge for Papa."

Her mother placed a bookmark in the volume she held and gave full attention. "What is it, Dear?"

Rising, she handed the Nugents' note to her mother and drew a sheet of paper from a compartment in the secretary. Concentrating, she selected a pen and ink.

Gwendolyn finished reading the note and raised her

eyes to Carrie's. "What were your father's orders?"

Inside, Carrie's spirit wilted at the word *orders*. Yes, they were orders. Worst of all, she must bring the note back for Papa's approval. He trusted her with nothing.

But what of her own dilemma? She was sure the Nugents' note had to do with the embarrassment involving Trouble, Graham Nugent, and herself. She wondered what the man intended to accomplish.

Was the invitation sent to bring them together again, or was it sent to insult her through her family? Papa's views on religion were public knowledge. None of the family had ever attended church.

Papa hated the church, and her feelings matched his. She didn't actually hate it; she only despised the way people acted when they were not in church. Graham Nugent, for instance. He and his family went to church, yet had he cared for her discomfort and hurt? Not as far as she could tell. Suddenly alert, she realized her mother had spoken to her.

"Carrie. Carrie, are you listening?"

Through with woolgathering, Carrie shook her head and glanced at her mother. "I'm sorry, Mama." She sighed and addressed the blank sheet of paper again. "Papa's orders were to answer the note and bring it back to him. He wants to read it before it's sent. He wasn't happy to be invited." She hoped her mother might take exception and ventured further. "Actually, he took the invitation as an insult."

"Then simply reply that we are otherwise engaged,"

her mother stated calmly and opened her book again.

Not a satisfactory resolution to Carrie, but she wrote the note twice, then a third time for neatness, and took it back to her father. Accepting her message, he closed it with his wax and seal and told her to have Trouble take it to the Nugent home at once. Carrie left in search of him.

Passing by the dining room, she saw activity related to their family's Christmas Eve party, but even that failed to uplift her dismal mood. Curiosity about the Nugents' party filled her mind, and she found herself wishing she could attend. That was very strange. She had no idea from which part of her imagination the thought sprang.

In the barn, she climbed the ladder to the loft where she found Trouble, and she settled onto a mound of hay. Wiping perspiration from his face, he hung his pitchfork on the wall and flopped down in the straw beside her.

Carrie brushed a bit of straw off his shoulder. "Did you throw down enough hay for Samantha too?"

He drew back, frowning. "You don't think I'd feed Bandy and not feed her, do you?" he asked as if she had genuinely offended him.

"No, of course not, Trouble. Forgive me. I know what a responsible person you are." She reached under her cloak, and from the bodice of her blue wool dress, she handed him the note she had written. "Papa would like you to take this to the Nugent home."

Excited, Trouble sat up straight. "Mr. Nugent's house!" he said with a smile. "What does it say, Carrie? Did he tell you what he was writing about?"

"Don't get your hopes up. It's not what you think. It's a reply Papa had me write refusing their invitation to a Christmas Eve party at their home." Carrie raised her chin and said as stiffly as she could manage, "I wish I could have added a few distinguishing remarks to young Mr. Nugent, but I hadn't the chance."

"Oh, Carrie, you shouldn't. . ."

Carrie stood and brushed straw from her cloak. "Don't try to read the note. You might break the seal. Now I have to get inside and help Mama and Cook prepare dinner. You can help me put more candles on the Christmas tree afterwards. Go! Hurry now, and don't take time to talk. Papa might hear of it, and he'd be very angry."

"I wish we weren't having our family dinner the same night, so we could attend their party," Trouble said, only half listening to her warning. "I'd like to go. I like Mr. Nugent, and I want to see him again. I'd like to go to the church program too.

"The Sanderson twins are in a play they're giving. They told me all about it. They're going to be shepherds, and they're going to lead a pet lamb. It's a story about a baby and a stable. Virgie and Conrad went to a play once in Baltimore. We've never done anything like that." Trouble hardly paused.

"And that's not all I'd like to do, Carrie. I'd like to see the inside of the Community Church. Four of the boys I know go there, and I want to know why they like it so much. Doesn't that make you curious?"

The more Trouble talked, the sorrier Carrie felt for

him. The yearning in his voice touched her heart and brought tears to her eyes. It didn't seem fair that he should be kept from going to the church program. He had no feelings against the church. It was unfair of her parents to pass their objections on to him.

"Trouble," she said, her arm around his shoulders, "someday when you grow up, you'll be able to make choices of your own. No one will be able to tell you what to do. Among other things, you can go into a church anytime you like. Remember my problem, and don't let other people make your choices for you."

"I know what you're talking about, and I'll remember. I'll be different when I have children, Carrie. I'll let them make up their own minds about serious things."

Trouble helped her onto the loft ladder and followed her down. When they reached the bottom, he spoke again.

"Maybe when the family comes for our Christmas Eve party, we'll feel better."

She squeezed his arm. "I know we will. Go on now. If Papa sees us talking and you haven't gone, he'll be upset."

With a little wave and a lowered head, Trouble went to saddle Bandy. Carrie left the barn feeling sadder than she had after the scene with her father.

≈

On Christmas Eve, the older Warden children and their families drove through the cold night in carriages with brass lanterns lighting the way. Throughout the Warden house, the flicker of candles, decorated with evergreen, created an enchanting ambience, awaiting the family gathering.

Under the great tree in the living room, Carrie and Trouble had placed the homemade presents they'd spent weeks creating for members of the family. When the relatives added their presents, the mound of gifts would spread out and cover the floor at that end of the room.

What fun we'll have when Caleb and Joshua get here! Carrie mused. Both blond, her older brothers looked enough alike to be twins. They had the same number of children too: Caleb, two boys and a girl, and Joshua, two girls and a boy. All the children had blond hair too. Their wives, however, could not have been more different.

Caleb's wife, Eleanor, a tall, slender brunette, loved her family more than her life and practiced cooking as an art. She lacked the fragile beauty of Joshua's ginger-haired wife, but she had respect and sympathy for all creatures, and Carrie adored her.

When she thought of Letitia, she smiled. Joshua's wife was like a beautiful butterfly in flight, never lighting in one place long enough to be captured. Her children loved her because she played with them almost every time they asked, and consequently her tiny home suffered. But Joshua did not seem to mind the clutter, so Carrie loved both women because they made her brothers happy.

Virgie and Conrad arrived late; their fancy buggy had skidded into a ditch and cracked a wheel. Stout Conrad, not a rider, cajoled the horse into town to fetch another conveyance while Virgie shivered under several quilts in the cold buggy. Her husband spent the entire evening complaining of the unlikelihood of locating a wheelwright on Christmas Day.

"I think one of the men at the mill can be called into service," Mortimer said. "I'll send a servant to tell him later. You and Virgie will have to spend the night."

"Won't the man resent coming to fix the wheel on Christmas Day?" Conrad asked.

Flashing a surprised glance at him, Mortimer declared, "What difference does that make? He'll do as he's told, or he'll be without a job."

Conrad had no reply, and the children, clamoring for their parents' attention, broke the silence.

Crawling around the glistening tree and giggling with them, Carrie helped the little ones search for presents marked with their names. Some were wrapped in cloth, some in paper saved all year for this honor, and some in leftover bits of wallpaper. Bright ribbons, bias cut by Carrie and hemmed by Mama, festooned each wrapping. So attractive were they that the adults also sneaked a peek at the presents tagged with their names.

Leaving Trouble to entertain the children, Carrie joined the women, setting food on the buffet and the long dining room table. She had arranged ornaments of holly and pinecones threaded with red ribbons on the brass candelabra. Much as she disliked sewing, she had sewn a long row of shiny buttons down the center of the scarlet ribbons.

Carrie placed an extra stack of linen napkins on the sideboard. "Girls, don't you think Mama looks beautiful in her black bombazine now that it's trimmed in the green grogram? I had to beg her to wear it. She thinks it too formfitting."

"Oh, no, Mother Warden," objected Letitia. "It's perfect!"

Eleanor agreed, and Virgie chided, "Mother, I doubt you've gained an ounce in years. You're always busy." She moved aside a sponge cake on the buffet so she could fit in a pan of cinnamon rolls. "I must say, you've outdone yourself on the food this year. It all looks delicious."

"Well, with Carrie's help, Cook and I think it did turn out well. Of course, Carrie's never satisfied until we decorate every dish."

Letitia came from the kitchen with a bowl of hot beets. "I failed to mention that you look very nice tonight too, Carrie. I imagine your little blue gown is sure to impress one party in particular."

Bewildered, Carrie stopped. *What a strange thing to say.*

Her father entered the room, and he and her mother spoke together in whispers on their way to the kitchen. *There's another peculiar thing.* Carrie noticed their strained expressions when they came back, and Mortimer commented loudly on the food.

"This is a meal fit for a king! Much better, I expect, than the food at the Nugent party tonight. Maybe some of you don't know, but we got an invitation. I expect you've surmised how I answered that." Slyly, Mortimer stroked his whiskers. "Took me only a minute to reject that offense, I can tell you."

"We got one too, Papa Warden, but we were coming here," Letitia said with a tinge of regret.

"So did we," chorused Virgie and Eleanor.

So it was not meant as a threat or a taunt. Carrie felt jubilant. He. . .they invited everyone in the family. The evening was getting better and better. She was having new thoughts about Graham Nugent, and she moved toward the French doors to slip out for a moment alone to absorb them.

But Papa spoke again. "Gwendolyn says we are ready to eat. Girls, I suggest you take your children to the table set up for them in the kitchen. They can go ahead, and the rest of us will wait for the Rafters. They should be here any minute."

Aware that everyone in the room was watching, Carrie felt her face grow warm, and she wanted to run from the room. *How mean!* They knew how she looked forward to this delightful evening with her family, and now it was ruined. Christmas with the children was ruined! Suddenly things made sense. Letitia thought she liked Rafter!

As her father promised, all three Rafters bustled into the entry hall minutes later. Alfred apologized with what Carrie thought the lamest of excuses, especially when their hostess had prepared such a splendid holiday feast.

"We would have been here sooner, but Ermagene

couldn't find the exact ribbon for her hair," he said, giving his hat to the maid and smoothing his thin gray hair and goatee.

Portly Mistress Rafter, smiling over his head, offered her explanation. "We must have the ensemble complete, must we not, Ermagene?"

Ermagene giggled her reply as the guests were hurried into the dining room. Seated between Alfred Rafter and his mother, with Ermagene across from her, Carrie felt miserable and betrayed and had no appetite at all.

What would it have been like tonight as the Nugents' guest? Was she a fool and Trouble right? Could there still be a chance for her?

She remembered the mixture of emotions that swept Graham Nugent's face as he kept Trouble's secret. He felt her brother's anguish. What kind of a man was he? A man who agonized over a boy's loyalty as well as his own. A man much different from her father.

Mr. Nugent was a church member, Trouble said. That would have to be dealt with. Also to be dealt with was the obvious. Alfred Rafter seemed accepted by her family as her future husband. Running away offered the only alternative unless. . .

six

Christmas morning dawned cold but with a clear blue sky full of sunshine. Because the family had stayed late, so had the Rafters. Later, offering sleeping apparel, filling the water pitcher, and seeing to their convenience, Carrie had relieved her mother of settling Virgie and Conrad in for the night.

She had gone to her own bed physically and mentally exhausted. In the morning, she felt everyone in the family would be glad last night lay behind them.

Papa and Mama were still asleep. Not a sound came from Trouble's room either; he was probably extra tired. Last night's stress had worn on his nerves too. Carrie slipped out quietly to ride by herself.

Not troubling her groom, she saddled Samantha herself to exercise the frisky mare. Samantha stamped the ground in anticipation of her morning workout. Carrie was on her back in seconds, and the mare scampered away, responding to the gentle heel of her mistress. Carrie needed fresh air to clear her head. There was much to consider.

Papa had announced that the mills would be closed today, after his workers "whined and begged" to have Christmas Day off again—with the exception of the man assigned to repair the wheel of Conrad's buggy. To Carrie the workers' request did not seem excessive. Papa would not have to pay them, and the villagers deemed the day so important that losing a day's wages didn't seem to matter.

If the employees were poor because of all the children they had, or so Papa said, how could they give up a day's wages so easily? For some mythical story about a baby born in a stable? Trouble had latched onto the same story. Why was everyone so fascinated?

She breathed a sigh and sat up straight in the saddle to give her appearance all the aid at her command. Her riding habit had weathered the water stain that dampened it when she escaped from Graham Nugent. A good brushing and pressing had returned it to its normal, aged best.

Carrie had hoped to receive a new riding habit for Christmas, but it never materialized. In fact, Mr. Rafter and his mother held forth dramatically on the subject of "female riders moving out and about in public." Her parents were quick to agree, so no new habit. It was the latest in the Rafters' string of complaints regarding her demeanor.

Thoughts of last night's fiasco broke the spell of the peaceful December morning. For her, the evening had plunged into an abyss upon the arrival of the Rafters. She had been the focus of their attention from the time they entered the house.

"You're looking very lovely in that blue gown, Miss

Warden. It certainly becomes you," Alfred Rafter gushed when they were seated together at the dining table.

His huge mother contradicted his statement immediately. "I think young women should dress in more conservative shades, myself."

Seated farther down the table, Eleanor, who never took a stand against an older woman, entered the conversation with zeal. "Surely nothing could be more apropos than applying the spectrum of color to a lovely young girl's wardrobe. Perhaps she might even encourage others whose apparel lacks the radiance of her tasteful choices."

Seeing the flush of irritation on Eleanor's face, her husband, Caleb, regarded her outburst with awe. Carrie had never seen Caleb in a state of shock, and she smiled inwardly as her big brother beamed. He was proud of Eleanor!

Eleanor eyed Mistress Rafter with a steady gaze, not so much as glancing at Ermagene. But since the girl's carefully chosen pink hair bow had failed to rescue the drab wrenlike dress she wore, Eleanor's point was obvious.

For that one moment in time, at least, Carrie felt she had a friend who recognized the pressure being placed upon her. However, that had been the only consideration shown her in the Warden home all night.

Both Ermagene and Mistress Rafter took every opportunity to correct her or to find fault, and Mr. Rafter had approved. It had been an unbearable evening. Her knuckles whitened as she gripped Samantha's reins. *Papa simply must reconsider. He must!*

Approaching hoofbeats startled her; and from the corner of her eye, she caught a glimpse of Graham Nugent on his black steed. Undecided what to do, she did nothing, and he caught up with her.

"Good morning! Merry Christmas!" he called, his magnetic blue eyes brightening his wide smile. He stopped and faced her.

"Good morning, Mr. Nugent," she replied, though she barely had breath to liberate the words.

"I'm glad to see you. I have something for you," he said, reaching inside his jacket. He brought out a flat package and handed it to her. "This belongs to you. I found your hat and took it home. My mother has a friend who makes hats. Yours was soiled, so her friend cleaned it and replaced the feather with a new one. I hope you approve." He examined her face for any sign of exception.

Carrie took the package and unfolded it with trembling fingers. Embarrassed before him yet again, she replied, "That was very good of your mother. Would you thank her for me?" Taking out the little archer's hat, she smiled with pleasure at its look of renewal and put it on. Raising her lashes, she found his gaze concentrated on her. "Is it straight?"

Glad to be asked, he pinched the point of the crown. "Exactly right," he said, settling the reins in his gloved hand on the saddle. "Since you've decided to speak to me after all, for which I'm very grateful, would you do me the honor of riding with me this morning?"

Carrie felt an unnatural glow. "Perhaps we should forget the way we met and start anew." She raised her head and smiled into his eyes, reveling in his delighted expression. "A quarrel on a morning like this would be inexcusable, don't you agree?"

"I certainly do. Let's see," he said, pointing ahead. "We can go on either side of this tree, or I can drop behind. Promise you won't run away?" At Carrie's giggle, he let her go ahead and then followed.

Graham picked up the conversation again as they rode abreast. "I'm sorry you and your family couldn't be with us last night for our party. We had a wonderful program at church, and most of the congregation came to our house afterwards. The ladies brought food to add to what mother and her helpers had already prepared, and we had enough for the whole town."

"I'm sure it was very nice. Of course, we had a good time at our party too," Carrie said, trying to sound enthusiastic.

"That's good. Tell me about it. Was your family all together?"

"Yes, including the children. My brothers, Caleb and Joshua, have three children apiece. They are such sweet children, and Trouble is so good with them, even Joshua's baby. She's just beginning to walk."

Graham smiled and led the way along the bank of a brook they had chanced upon. "Travis is a fine boy. I found him mannerly and extremely thoughtful. Your parents should be very proud of him. So should you," he added.

"I am, believe me. He's my favorite of all the family."

"Would you be surprised to learn he said the same thing about you?"

The warmth in Carrie's face rose. "Mr. Nugent—"

"Graham."

She smiled. "All right, Graham. Now, over that next mound is a field Samantha loves to graze when she gets the chance. Shall we have a run?"

"Yes, but first let's water the horses."

The animals drank sufficiently; and when their owners urged them to a run, both seemed to enjoy the race. Samantha was no match for the tall black, but she did her best and followed Carrie's handling well. The horses grazed, and for the next hour the couple walked and rode, getting better acquainted.

When they turned back toward town, Carrie heard church bells in the distance. "Aren't they pretty? I love hearing the bells ring."

"Yes, I enjoy them too. That deep-throated bell belongs to the church my parents and I attend. We're having a special service this morning. I was enjoying your company so much I'm afraid I forgot the time." He stopped Raven and turned to her. "Carrie, why don't you come with me to church this morning? The choir will sing, and we'll hear the Christmas story from the Book of Luke. Won't you come with me?" Graham looked as if he expected her to agree immediately.

Carrie knew her father would never forgive her. "I can't go with you, Mr. Nugent. I—"

"Graham. My name is Graham."

Frustrated, she started again. "Graham, I don't attend church. My father. . .uh, we don't favor churchgoing."

Graham's kind face filled with concern. "God loves you, Carrie. Don't you sense something greater out there than what we see on earth?"

"I'm not sure what that means. Papa—"

"Turning to God is a choice no one else can make for you, Carrie. The Christmas story is about how God sent Jesus to earth to bring men to Himself. He gave us a plan. Please come and hear it with me."

Fear seized her. Of what, she did not know. She only knew she had to get away. Though Graham captivated her, his presence plagued her with a feeling that deep down inside she lacked something. Something important. What was it? What did she not have?

"No! Please. I cannot go!" she cried.

Turning Samantha, she kicked the horse and sped away through a grove of young trees.

"Wait! Carrie, wait!" Graham called after her in vain.

The mare, confused by her handling and another voice, tried to jump a small thicket, and Carrie slid awkwardly off her back. Rushing forward, Graham grabbed Samantha's reins and tied both horses to a sapling.

"Carrie, are you hurt?" he said, bending down to her, his face etched with worry.

Crying, she pointed to her foot. "I've hurt my—"

"Here, let me take your boot off."

"No!" She tried to rise but could not. "You must go to my home and have Papa bring the carriage." She gasped in pain but went on. "Say as little as possible about our meeting, but go!"

"I'm sorry, little one. I have no intention of leaving you here alone. If you won't let me find out how badly you're hurt, you must allow me to do what I think best." He knelt beside her and lifted her in his arms. "If you'll put your arms around my neck, I can carry you more easily," he said.

She obeyed, and he carried her to Raven and settled her on his back. He brought Samantha around, passed her reins to Carrie, and took off his jacket. Folded, it padded her leg.

"You guide Samantha. We'll keep to a moderate gait and ride to my home, where my mother can attend you. She is an excellent nurse." He climbed up on the gelding behind her.

"But I can't go home with you. It wouldn't be right. Papa—Graham, you must take me home."

"I'm taking you to my home because we are roughly four miles from your property. We are less than a mile from my home near the village."

Carrie supposed what he said made sense, but her father would never understand. Nevertheless, they were on their way.

She was tempted to relax against Graham's broad chest and sob out her pain, but she held her body rigid.

His arm, like a band of iron, supported her as they rode. She made herself ignore it, and her mind shifted again to her father. How would she ever explain her way out of this?

&a.

Graham pondered the same question. Mortimer Warden might never forgive the indiscretion of his being the one to rescue Carrie. In the meantime, he had to find a way to get her injury attended to and then deliver her home safely.

If his parents hadn't left for church yet, his mother would help. She had handled other crises with calm and good judgment. This would be no different—or would it?

The scent of lilac fragrance emanating from the small body in his arms enveloped him. As if that were not enough, her red-gold hair lay against his shoulder in beautiful tangles. He could reach out and crush a strand to his lips if he chose. With frequent glances, he observed the sober set of her mouth and wished he could kiss the worry away. He tore his mind from the dangerous thought at once.

It's not my job to figure out where this is going, Lord. I leave the outcome to You. I'll do the most appropriate thing You show me to do, but thank You for letting me hold her in my arms.

Graham wondered if he might someday tell Carrie of his prayer as they rode together to meet his mother.

seven

Mary Nugent opened the back door and cried, "Graham! Where have you been? We will be late to church, and you haven't even changed." She grabbed his arm and started to pull him inside.

"Wait, Mother! We have company." He pointed to Raven, who was still carrying his nervous passenger. Beside them, Samantha stamped the ground near a trellis covered with dormant wisteria vines.

Mary turned to her son, her face a question.

"She had an accident, Mother. She fell when her horse jumped a thicket, and her, uh, limb is hurt. I brought her here so you could have a look. She won't allow me to inspect it."

"I should certainly hope not! Carry her in, and I'll run and tell Riley to go on to church without me." She moved toward the parlor. "I'll be back to help you take her up to my room in just a few seconds."

Graham nodded in reply and strode out to Carrie. Smiling, he held out his arms to lift her down. "Are you ready for another trip? Mother will be right with you. She'll tend your injury upstairs in her bedroom."

"Oh, I'm going to be in such trouble," Carrie moaned.

Timidly, she placed her hands on his shoulders to be lowered. Graham noticed her wince with pain as he

73

lifted her from the horse, and he carried her quickly into the house.

His mother, waiting to greet them at the bottom of the stairs, had taken off her hat, coat, and gloves.

She approached Carrie. "My dear, I'm Mary Nugent. I'm sorry you were hurt. We'll do something to help you right away. It's a shame we have to meet under these circumstances, but let me assure you, you're very welcome in our home."

"Thank you. I'm sorry to cause all of you this difficulty."

"Think nothing of it. I'm just glad Graham managed to get you here, so I can help."

Graham, losing patience with the conversation, interrupted. "Let me take her upstairs, Mother. She's trembling with pain." Secretly he hoped it was her reaction to being close to him. As for himself, he had trouble breathing, and it had nothing to do with climbing stairs. Holding her warmth so close was clearly unreasonable punishment.

Mary went ahead of them. "We'll be there in just a moment, Carrie, and, Graham, you must stay. Her boot will have to be cut off. After a closer look, I can see how swollen the injury has become."

In Graham's mind merged all the emotions of the moment. He believed God's leading affirmed the day's events. Not that he believed God had caused the accident, but because of Carrie's impulsive dash to get away, He had brought them to an amenable result. There was every chance for a closer association.

His concern now focused on the extent of her injury

and the repercussions she would suffer when her family learned who had rescued her from the grove. Mortimer Warden would be furious that Carrie had run into him, and he still had no ideas on how to explain their being together.

In her room, his mother spread the bed with a clean sheet, and Graham gently laid Carrie on it. Seeming ashamed of her tears, Carrie covered her face with her hands. Graham wanted to gather her in his arms again to let her cry herself out.

On a table beside the bed, Mary placed a tray of items she needed to tend the leg and spoke softly to Carrie. "My dear, I feel your need for privacy, but I must insist that you let Graham cut the boot off your limb. We can see that the swelling is growing worse; and if we don't cut the boot away immediately, you may have complications. I promise you I will hold your habit down around you until the boot is cut; then my son will leave the room."

Carrie's hands came down as Mary talked, and she nodded, glancing only once at Graham. "Thank you."

With a sharp knife from his father's workshop, Graham split the soft boot open; and with a last dismal look back at Carrie, he went out and shut the door behind him.

Mary took the boot away and examined Carrie. "I've seen this before. You have some pulled ligaments." She ran her fingers all around the leg and ankle. She had a light touch, yet Carrie felt as if a doctor were examining her. "Though your injury is discolored and swollen, I feel no broken bones. We'll have you feeling better in no time."

She cleansed the exposed skin, then bound the entire lower leg with a bundle of white muslin strips. Carrie felt relief from the pressure right away and relaxed. But she couldn't walk. Just having her foot hang down without support made the pain greater.

What now? How would Papa treat the incident, and how would he treat her? Tears came back, but they were tears of the vanquished. Papa would not take her being with Graham lightly. She would never hear the end of the fact that she had ridden her horse with another man while being promised to Rafter. Her turmoil must have shown because Mary questioned her.

"Carrie, are you all right?"

"Yes, I just. . ."

Mary waited a few seconds, then placed a chair close to the bed. "I'm ready to listen if you want to talk about anything."

Carrie wished she could pour out her heart to this kind lady. She was the kind of mother, tender and understanding, that she longed for. But there would be no understanding at the Warden household. Her mother would stand by her father's decision.

Carrie looked into Mary's sympathetic eyes. "I wouldn't know where to start."

"Maybe at the beginning?" said the older woman.

"There's no place to begin. It's such a muddle."

Mary reached for the tray on the table and brought it to her lap. "Does the muddle have anything to do with my son?"

Carrie nodded. "He is the main difficulty. You see, my

little brother wanted. . .he wanted to keep me from being pledged to. . .to a man I don't—"

A knock sounded at the door, and Carrie turned a desperate face to Mary Nugent.

"Mother, are you through yet?" Outside the door, Graham's voice sounded tight and anxious. "Is Carrie all right? Tell me something, please."

Mary placed her hand on Carrie's to silence her. "I have the wrapping finished. She has pulled some ligaments. Your father rode his horse to church, so if you will hitch up the buggy, you and I will take Carrie home."

"Excellent!" he said. "I knew I could depend on you! I hoped we could have lunch, but I'm sure this is best. I shouldn't be more than a few minutes."

As his footsteps retreated, Mary Nugent smoothed the hand she held. "Don't think that muddles can't be worked out, Carrie. God has answers we haven't yet dreamed of."

❧

All the way home, bundled in a warm quilt in the Nugents' buggy, Carrie felt she had never been so happy. Nor had she ever been treated with such deference. She felt important to the two people in the conveyance, who talked to her over their shoulders from the front seat.

"Mother convinced me this is the best way to handle the explanation for your accident, Carrie. With her along, it will seem perfectly natural that we helped you," asserted Graham.

Carrie wasn't so easily convinced. Happy as she was, she believed her father would circumvent any explanation, see right into her heart, and get at the truth. She felt she fairly glowed with her secret. She and Graham had ridden together for three hours, and she would never forget it.

When she looked up, Graham was gazing back at her with the warmest of expressions. "Are you warm enough back there? Mother, maybe we should have brought another quilt. She mustn't catch cold."

Before Carrie could protest, Mary Nugent set him straight. "Why don't you give the child time to answer, Graham? Carrie, my dear, are you cold?"

"No, I'm fine. Just enjoying the conversation."

"You see?" Mary adjusted her hat and pushed a large handbag aside with her foot so she could turn farther toward Carrie. "Now, you two, I think it would be better if you let me carry the thread of thought when we get to the Wardens'. I may as well tell you right now that I intend to get off the subject of the ride as soon as possible."

Carrie lowered her gaze. "I'd be grateful, Mistress Nugent. Papa complains that I ride too much as it is. I adore it, but if he finds out I rode with your son this morning, he will tighten the restrictions even more."

Both Nugents looked concerned.

"What do you mean?" asked Mary.

"Papa thinks if he withholds a new riding habit, for instance, I'll be ashamed of this one and not ride so much. Which reminds me, Mistress Nugent, I want to thank you for having my hat cleaned and pressed." She smiled at them both. "The hat is now the nicest part of the outfit."

"Pardon me for disagreeing with you, Miss Warden, but I think your little habit is very attractive on you," Graham said. "But I promise I won't mention it to your father," he added, smiling.

Staring down the road, Mary motioned toward an oncoming wagon. "Look! There's the Marakov family. I wonder what they're doing out here? They always come to the service at church on Christmas Day."

Graham frowned. "Looks like they didn't make it today."

"Stop the horses, Graham. Let's see if anything's wrong."

Graham called out to the horses and steered the buggy to the side of the road. The other conveyance, containing several children, approached and stopped adjacent to the buggy.

"Merry Christmas!" the children yelled, waving and smiling.

"Merry Christmas to you!" returned Graham and Mary.

A little girl about four years old tumbled out of the wagon and came running to Mary's side of the buggy. "Hello, Francie," Mary said, helping the child up on her lap and giving her a hug. "Are you folks out for a drive?" she called to those in the wagon when Francie settled down.

"No," answered a tall, husky man whom Carrie supposed to be the father. "We're on our way home from work!" The crowd in the wagon laughed uproariously.

"It was supposed to be work," said a boy a little older than Trouble.

Taking up the gleeful tale, a younger girl with tawny

hair said, "But we found a haystack! We slid down it a hundred times!"

On Mary's lap, little Francie piped up. "We petted the baby cows too. They were eatin' that sticky pile we slid down."

Squeals and laughter emanated from the wagonload of children, each shouting a different version of the experience. The man quieted them and turned to smile at the woman seated beside him.

Shifting the baby she held to one side, she shushed the children again. "We couldn't have Pa's need to work spoiling our celebration of the Lord's birthday. We had to be together!"

The man, Marakov, explained in a European accent, "That's right. We planned to be in church this morning, but my boss at the mill sent for me last night and told me to be here at sunup. I had to fix a busted wheel on his son's carriage." He chuckled and added, "And when that man says to be somewhere at sunup, you better be there."

All the adults except Carrie laughed at his joke. In her mind, there was no doubt who had given the order. It was Papa. She wondered how the children's sliding down the haystack might affect Papa. If they had disturbed the hay enough to let moisture get inside the stack and ruin it, he would remember the Marakovs and relieve the man of his job.

To keep out of sight, she scrunched down in the seat as far as she could. So far, the Nugents hadn't put the details together. She didn't recognize the man and woman in the wagon, but they would recognize her because she was

Mortimer Warden's daughter. Carrie pulled the quilt up to hide her face and kept perfectly still.

Doesn't anyone like Papa? She was beginning to think no one did. What he had done to her, promising her to a man as old as himself, he had done on a different level to many others, and with the same arrogance. She had known it all her life. This latest indignity was an expression of his power.

The poor man had done as he was told. How did he get out here? Had the family come with him and stayed? Or had they brought him out and camped in the hayfield so the children wouldn't disturb the "Royal" Wardens? In seconds she heard Graham ask the same question.

"I'm Graham Nugent, Mr. Marakov. Do you remember me?"

Carrie caught a glimpse of Marakov taking off his fur hat. "Sure, sure. I remember you. You're a big city lawyer now."

Graham chuckled. "Well, maybe not too big yet, but I believe God will make of me what He wants someday."

Marakov paused a few seconds. "Mistress Nugent, I think your boy has a good head. As long as he puts his faith in the Lord, he'll be all he can be."

"How did you get out to your boss's home, Sir? Has your family been on the road, back and forth, all morning?" Graham asked.

"No, our oldest son brought me out this morning on his way to his wife's family. They will celebrate with that family today instead of us." Sadness edged the man's voice. "But. . .it makes no difference!" He laughed.

"Now we will have our happy celebration!"

The children in the wagon squealed, and Graham encouraged them to be on their way. Mary handed Francie down, and the child ran to her family. As the wagon rumbled past, hands waved good-byes, and only the toddler saw Carrie peeking from her hiding place.

Mary turned to Carrie immediately. "Are you all right, Dear? Not too cold?"

"No, I'm fine," Carrie answered, too embarrassed to say anything else.

Though they didn't know the circumstances of the night before, she suspected the Nugents guessed the identity of the man who'd changed this special day's plans for the Marakovs.

Graham slapped the reins for more speed. "We'll have you home in a few minutes, Carrie." He glanced over his shoulder at her. "I think it best that we say nothing of meeting the Marakovs this morning."

How sensitive he is. Mary too. It was obvious they knew what had happened, and they sensed from her silence that they should not introduce her to the Marakovs.

What must it be like to belong to a family so in harmony they spoke to each other without words?

eight

Surprisingly, Graham and his mother received a cordial welcome from Mortimer and Gwendolyn Warden.

"My sakes, Carrie, what's happened to you?" her father asked, so awed by the sight he left them standing outside. Finally realizing his error, he motioned them inside with both hands. "Come in, come in!"

Her mother wrung her hands. "Oh, Carrie, Dear, your le—limb! You're hurt!"

"Gwendolyn, will you get out of the way? Step back and let them in." As usual, her father intended to handle the incident.

"What happened?" he demanded, looking at Graham.

"She fell from her horse," said Mary Nugent, interrupting as she stepped inside the door. "I think we should take her someplace where she can lie down, Mr. Warden."

Embarrassed, Mortimer sputtered, "Of course. Would you take her upstairs to her room?"

The couple, expressing shock at Carrie's fragile appearance, followed behind as Graham carried their daughter up the stairs.

"We haven't introduced ourselves. I'm Mistress Riley Nugent, and this is my son, Graham." Mary also explained the accident on the way, making sure they understood the tryst was entirely aboveboard. "I thought it fortunate Graham was out riding in the area. He fetched Carrie to our house."

They reached the upper floor, and Gwendolyn held the door while Graham carried his lovely charge inside and placed her on the chaise lounge. No sooner had he done so than her father asked the exact question Carrie had dreaded.

"How did you happen to fall from your horse, Carrie? It's not like you. With all the time you spend on that animal, you surely are a better rider than that."

Carrie answered honestly. "I don't know, Papa. One minute I was jumping a thicket, and the next I had fallen to the ground with my limb crumpled under me." Five pairs of eyes gazed upon her, including those of Trouble, who had trailed behind.

With a look more mischievous than sympathetic, he quipped, "You're very lucky Mr. Nugent went out this morning and found you."

His grin challenged whoever cared to guess his secret. Carrie felt like strangling him. She glanced at Graham in distress. Aware the truth could be read in Trouble's expression, she felt her liberation when Graham changed the subject.

"Mr. Warden," he said, "Father tells me your mills are working at top speed this winter. That's certainly good news for the community. It appears we will have an ample supply of flour and cornmeal for the storage bins."

Mortimer Warden, glad of a respite from the feminine discussion of his daughter's health, turned to face Graham. "Yes, business is good. Why don't we find a couple of comfortable chairs downstairs in the parlor and have some coffee? I'd enjoy a cup if you agree, and we can occupy ourselves with less feminine subjects."

Carrie watched gratefully as Graham followed her father from the room.

Amazed that Papa had received the Nugents so well, she relaxed and repositioned her leg for greater comfort. Lying back, she let go the stress of the last few minutes. Trouble's remark had almost ruined the day, but it was likely to be forgotten in the men's conversation.

"This is such a lovely room, Mistress Warden," Mary Nugent said. "I've always been fond of yellow, and I see someone here likes it as well. Which of you did the decorating? Or did you do it together?"

Gwendolyn's modest smile negated the compliment. "The colors actually were a matter of combining our tastes, I believe. Isn't that true, Carrie? Except for the yellow. It's not my favorite, but she insisted that be the basic color. The rest became a matter of matching the right materials together."

As she talked, her mother moved around the room as though rediscovering it, and Carrie wondered if she had been too austere with her privacy. Had she not been, would she and her mother have been closer? The time spent with Mary Nugent had been a revelation of what a mother and daughter relationship should be. Perhaps she was at fault. She should have done more to build her mother's confidence. Maybe then they'd share the bond Mary and her son enjoyed.

Carrie remembered Mary's soft voice encouraging her through the pain of having her leg tended. Their conversation had been so unaffected that the temptation to ask her advice had surfaced more than once. Yet she'd let it go. Now that the time was past, Carrie wished she hadn't.

She wondered how Mistress Nugent would advise an innocent, fated to wed a much older man. Would she disagree, or would she, like Gwendolyn, see no point in fighting it? Even with Mary Nugent's insight, it was possible she might look at the advantages of the match and dispense the same advice.

She didn't care. She could not abandon the promise to her grandmother that she would wait for a romantic man like her grandfather. She often took the box with the little key out of its hiding place to remind her of her grandparents' great love.

Today was Christmas Day, their special day, their wedding day. Grandmother Lawrence's words lingered, calling forth a longing in Carrie's heart. Though her father didn't believe in God, she hoped, as her grandmother had believed, that one man would come along to love her for a lifetime. When he appeared, she would give him the little key representing the key to her heart.

Her feelings toward Graham had changed drastically. She'd dared suppose he might be the one. If he weren't, and she had to marry Rafter, she'd throw the key away before presenting it to the unwanted suitor. But she was determined to wait as long as possible for a romantic man, like her grandfather or Graham Nugent, to claim her heart.

Drawing her cloak around her slender form, Mary Nugent moved toward the door. "Carrie, Dear, we must leave now. If your parents will allow us, Graham and I will come back in a day or two to see how you are progressing. Do you think we might do that, Mistress Warden?"

"Oh, I'm sure it will be acceptable," her mother replied. "Let's go down now and find out what day is best for Mortimer." With that, she turned quickly, motioned Mary ahead of her, and opened the door.

Carrie noted the other woman's puzzled look. *She must wonder why Papa has to be present when the Nugents come to visit.* Anyone would wonder. Little did Mary know it was Papa's permission that her mother really sought. She would do nothing without his agreement.

Mistress Nugent probably never heard of such a thing as a husband's permission. In her home, she received the same respect in her daily life that her husband did. *What a difference!* At the Warden house, honoring Papa's wishes merely kept the peace.

Carrie didn't realize Trouble had stayed in the room after the others left until he bobbed up, grinning, from behind the window seat curtain.

"You like Graham after all, don't you?"

"Trouble! You frightened me. Do you realize what

difficulty you could have caused if Papa caught your cruel little joke? If Graham hadn't changed the subject, Papa would have understood what you were hinting."

"He wasn't even listening. I could tell. He was bored no end with Mama and Mistress Nugent fussing over you. You didn't answer, Carrie. You like Mr. Nugent, don't you?"

"I thought you'd gone downstairs, Trouble, but since you're here, would you please bring me another pillow for my back? I want to be able to look out the window. It's such a beautiful day."

Trouble brought a pillow from her cedar chest at the foot of the bed. "Now, is that going to be high enough, or do you need another one so you can prop yourself up higher? You know you don't want to miss seeing Mr. Nugent leave." His impish voice and sly expression teased Carrie unmercifully.

"Trouble, you're dreadful. I want no such thing. It's just a lovely day, and I want to be able to see outside. Pull the curtains back too, why don't you? I may want to read later."

Trouble gave her another puckish look and ran out of the room. Where was he going? When her brother was in his trouble mood, there was no telling what he'd do. She straightened the pillow behind her back while she waited and tried not to expect the worst.

Seconds later, he clumped up the stairs with the sound of heavier footfalls following. Carrie knew instantly what he had done. She heard soft voices down the hall and quickly smoothed her hair. Her hat—it was gone. *Oh, no! Not again!*

At the door, Trouble offered a playful smile, and Graham appeared in the doorway behind him. "I told them you wanted to thank Mr. Nugent for rescuing you," he said, obviously proud of his strategy.

"Thank you indeed, Mr. Nugent. I hope you know how much I appreciate your help," she said, giving their covert conduct at least one honest moment. "I don't know what would have happened if you hadn't taken me home to your mother. Her quick treatment kept the injury from becoming worse."

"You're very welcome, Miss Warden, and I remind you again, my name is Graham." He pulled his gaze from hers to observe the bandaged foot. "Are you feeling better now? More comfortable at least?"

"Yes, I'm in much less pain now. Thank you." She smiled up at him. "I like your mother, Graham. She's a wonderful lady. I've never met anyone like her, and I have a feeling I share that opinion with others."

"You're right. Mother always seems to do the right thing. She's the most devout Christian I've ever known. My father and I often remark that we are blessed by God to be related to her."

Anxiously Trouble took Graham's hand. "Come on, Mr. Nugent. We have to get out of here. Papa went out to get a cedar log for the fireplace, and he'll be back any second. He'll be mad as a hornet if he finds out I brought you upstairs. He'd rather Carrie write a thank-you note instead of having you visit her personally—in her room."

Graham gripped his hat in his hands. "You're right, Trouble. Your father and I are on fair terms right now. I don't want to do anything to spoil it." He gave Carrie an intimate smile. "Please, get well soon so we can ride together." He started toward the door, then turned, grinning. "Oh, and I have your hat. Again."

Not understanding the banter between the two, Trouble resorted to nagging. "Come on, Mr. Nugent!"

"Yes, go!" Carrie pleaded, though she wanted him to stay. As he went out the door, she added a deliberate request to make him look back. "Thank your mother again for me." She tilted her head. "And thank you, Graham, for guarding my lovely hat."

He smiled and left, and Carrie felt the day darken. What were these feelings? She knew. Though they had known each other only a few days, Graham was more than an acquaintance. A true bond was developing between them.

She liked his mother so much. Mary Nugent had turned a potential debacle into a friendly afternoon visit. She hoped the time would come when she could tell Mary Nugent how much her trust meant to her.

What made Mistress Nugent so wonderful? Graham called her a "devout Christian." But she was so different from the Christians Carrie knew. While the subject of Christianity aroused no interest within her family, she had a definite feeling that Graham yearned to discuss the subject with her.

Glancing out the window, she saw the Nugents' buggy

speeding toward the crossroads, and she speculated on the possibility of future meetings between Graham Nugent and herself.

Suddenly, and without turning, Graham lifted his arm in a slight farewell wave as if he knew who would be watching.

nine

Her father elaborated on the details of Carrie's accident to the Rafters, after which she suffered further reproof from her intended and his mother.

"What a dreadful concern for your family, Miss Warden!" Mistress Rafter exclaimed, taking another tart from the silver tea tray Mortimer had ordered Cook to prepare. "As Alfred informed me of it, I just threw up my hands. I had anticipated a catastrophe if you kept riding that animal around the countryside. Did I not say that, Alfred, Dear?"

"Yes, you certainly did, Mother, and I agreed with you. As I told you before, Miss Warden, and as you have certainly proven, it is not seemly for a young, unmarried lady to ride a horse alone where any sort of cad might accost her." Aside from his words, Rafter's look also reproached Carrie.

From his chair in the parlor, Papa, silent and unsmiling, glared at Carrie. She felt like an injured lamb, lost on a rocky trail at a perilous height. No one came to her rescue. No one remembered that she was the one hurting.

Carrie's chaise lounge had been moved to the parlor for her comfort, but she was anything but comfortable. In truth, it was the pain in her heart that crushed her spirit more than her physical pain.

With the Rafters' afternoon visit, her parents had renewed their callous attitude. Alfred Rafter's social status took precedence over any misery inflicted upon their daughter. Now that his social status appeared on the brink of elevation, Papa gave no thought to his duty as a father. Only the unwanted arrangement secured his concentration.

Papa's wealth was considerable. He could afford a beautiful home and servants; yet when compared to the Rafter family's assets, it paled, and his envy knew no bounds. Mr. Rafter and his mother controlled a shipping business whose maritime trade routes constantly enriched their treasury.

Once she was married to Rafter, Papa would expect some of that wealth to rub off on him. The prospect shone like a diamond he could possess, and it hovered just out of his reach. With her marriage into the Rafter empire, he reasoned aloud, prospect would become possibility.

Carrie studied the grotesque threesome before her. If the suit Rafter wore had been on anyone else, Papa would have called him a dandy and forbade his entry into the house. There would have been no arranged marriage.

Made of expensive black wool, the suit nonetheless fit him horridly. Rafter was wider at the hip than at the shoulder, giving him a distinct pear shape. His stiff white shirt collar and mustard yellow tie clutched his neck like a strangler. The hapless garb, including the new-style derby hat he wore at his arrival, embarrassed her.

As for her own attire, with its overlapping flounces, Mistress Rafter reminded Carrie of a black barge floating on Chesapeake Bay. Ermagene's costume, a blue waist with leg-of-mutton sleeves and a green quilted skirt, was an equal disgrace. The idea of entering such a narrow-minded, tasteless family appalled her.

Gwendolyn rarely spoke; but in a moment of concern, she did try to soften the jabs at her daughter. "I believe Carrie to be an excellent rider. Ordinarily, she handles Samantha very well." She folded her hands daintily in her lap. "We must remember that an accident can befall anyone."

Her gaze swept Carrie's face, and Carrie answered with a surprised smile. Papa's eyes filled with contempt, and Carrie saw her mother's lashes lower defensively.

"Nevertheless, the result may be disastrous!" carped Rafter. "To others in town it will seem that she threw herself at a man who took her to his home in a very unorthodox manner. A shameful display!" he finished, and to Carrie his smile was not hateful. It was mean.

She could stand the abuse no longer. She had to fight back. "How can you be so unfeeling? I should think all of you would be glad Mr. Nugent took me to his home. Mistress Nugent had treated the same type of injury before and knew exactly what to do. I could not have been cared for more tenderly."

Her face burning with indignation, Carrie jerked the new crocheted throw over her legs. Though she tried to remain calm, her statement exposed her to ridicule, and her father's crimson face revealed the fury bottled inside. She was not moved. No matter what happened now, she had spoken the truth and was glad of it.

Ermagene, her eyes narrow, sat forward to choose an iced cookie from the tray. "Papa says losing one's temper is the most loathsome trait a young lady can exhibit. I should try to break myself of the habit if I were you. Papa will never stand for it in his house."

Carrie stared at the girl, astonished at her blatant statement, and, worse, in front of her father and mother. She sighed. *Why shouldn't she? She has no reason to think otherwise. Obviously, her family considers this hideous arrangement an understood fact.* Carrie wondered if anything could change her future. She saw herself on a downward slide into servitude and unhappiness.

Occupying the couch with Ermagene, Mistress Rafter wore an insidious smile that defined her deep-seated animosity toward Carrie. "Our little dear appreciates the social graces. Ermagene never gets herself into a position that would humiliate her father or me. She has been raised in a climate of agreement. It is beneath her to embarrass the family, I assure you. She loves and respects us too much."

"Yes, Grandmamma! I love and respect you and Papa so much," parroted Ermagene.

Although Mortimer seemed puzzled as to how to proceed, his gaze toward Carrie wore a softer expression. Carrie felt a ray of hope. Maybe things were not as desperate as they seemed. She wondered if he'd heard enough of his guests' insults to change his decision to trade her to Rafter to advance his business interests. In the next moment, however, her hopes were dashed.

Mortimer stuck his thumbs in the armholes of his vest

and threw out his chest. "I'm sure Carrie has learned her lesson. She's an intelligent girl and knows what's best for her. She will not want to see any of the Nugents again."

A knock at the door underscored the decree. Like a blanket, silence stifled the room's controversy. Light footsteps approached, and a maid entered and whispered to Gwendolyn. With a quick, discomfited glance around the parlor, Gwendolyn excused herself and slipped from the room. Mistress Rafter impatiently refilled her teacup herself, and pausing, cup in midair, she cocked her head at the sound of happy voices drifting from the hall.

With a flushed countenance, Carrie's mother reentered the parlor, trailed by Graham and Mistress Nugent. "Imagine my surprise! The Nugents came to inquire if Carrie has had any problems with her injury." Though her mother's panicky surveillance avoided her husband, she seemed to will him to handle this unexpected crisis.

The men stood; introductions and salutations were offered. Carrie, in a state of awe, simply observed. Compared to Rafter, Graham looked like Adonis. His wine jacket and waistcoat were tailored superbly to fit his broad shoulders; trousers of black gabardine accented his long legs and narrow hips. Smiling at the maid, he placed his black leather gloves in a black hat with a high crown and handed it to her.

Trouble jumped up from his stool at the checkerboard table and greeted them in a piping voice. "Hello, Mr. Nugent and, uh, Ma'am. I'm glad to see you! Maybe you can play a game of checkers with me, Mr. Nugent. No one around here is interested today."

Papa is as overwhelmed as I. Satisfied with Trouble's uninhibited greeting, Carrie hoped her genuine smile told the couple how welcome they were.

Despite his visible lack of pleasure at this intrusion, her father came to life and offered chairs for the new arrivals. Graham took one closest to Carrie, and his enveloping gaze made Carrie feel he yearned for the sight of her. Her face warmed with joy.

"I must say, Miss Warden, you look much better than the last time we saw you," Graham said. "You're not nearly so pale, and you seem to have come back to life. Don't you think so, Mother?"

"She seems decidedly different to my way of thinking." Mary Nugent set her reticule beside her chair and removed her gloves. "Do you rest well at night, Carrie?"

"Yes, I have no pain at night."

"And does the swelling diminish then?"

"Yes, it does. When I wake early in the morning, the pain's hardly noticeable. Though later. . ." Carrie forgot all but the two addressing her. "Mistress Nugent, I can't thank you enough for treating my injury so effectively. I didn't dream just binding it well would make that terrible pain go away." She looked at Graham. "You were both good to me, and I'll be grateful all my life."

Rafter bolted out of his chair. "I fear we must be going, Warden. It has become crowded and rather stuffy in the room. We'll leave you for a nice healthy ride in our carriage. Perhaps we can visit later when you have fewer guests. We must try not to tire our dearest Carrie," he hinted dramatically, drawing himself up into what he evidently thought a statuesque posture.

After an abrupt leave-taking to those in the room, the Rafters regrouped. Bidding the maid to fetch their coats and hats, they stamped toward the front entry, escorted by Gwendolyn, with Mortimer close behind whispering apologies.

In her happiness, Carrie didn't mind if she was overheard. "I'm so happy you came. Mother will order more tea when she gets back. Do stay for awhile. Please."

Trouble dragged a footstool close to the two visitors sitting near Carrie. His gaze focused on Graham, and Carrie was afraid he would monopolize the conversation when she wanted to talk to Graham herself.

Graham spoke first. "Tell me, young man, while your sister is indisposed, are you being the faithful brother by taking care of Samantha?"

"Yes," Trouble answered enthusiastically. "I keep her fed and watered and brushed. Each time I tend Bandy, I do the same for her. Carrie knows I wouldn't slight Samantha."

"Don't forget another important job," Graham said. "She's used to being ridden every day. I think you should borrow some of Bandy's time for Samantha. What do you think?"

Carrie saw another side of Graham Nugent. He had even given thought to the care of her beloved mare.

Trouble glanced from Graham to Carrie. "He's right, Carrie. I should have given Samantha a workout every day. I'm sorry I never thought of it."

Carrie reached out to him, and he clutched her hand. "I don't blame you, Trouble. There were plenty of people here who could have done it. They were never told by anyone to exercise Samantha, and that includes me."

Turning to Mary, she smiled, deliberately looking past Graham. "Your son seems a thoughtful, kind person, Mistress Nugent. Is he always thoughtful and kind, or is he really cranky at home and simply acting to impress us?"

Mistress Nugent laughed heartily. "I'm afraid I'm a poor judge. I'm far too biased for an objective opinion. To me he is a son any mother would be proud to claim. Not only is he thoughtful and kind, he has a very handsome face. Have you noticed?"

"Mother, will the two of you stop speaking of me as if I'm not in the room?" Graham complained. "It's disconcerting to a man."

The women and Trouble giggled at Graham's chagrin until Trouble rescued him by challenging him to a game of checkers.

Mary leaned forward and spoke softly to Carrie. "We have a gift for Travis, Carrie. Do you think we might give it to him while your parents are outside, talking with their guests? It's something personal."

Carrie saw the sincerity in her eyes and nodded. "I don't see why not."

"Then why don't I call him over before he and Graham start their game?"

Carrie's curiosity mounted. "Yes, go ahead. I can see this is important to you."

ten

"We brought you a gift, Trouble," Graham said, handing him the neat black Bible Mary took from her reticule. "For hundreds of years this book has been the guide for untold numbers of young people like you. I know you'll like it, and you'll be surprised how quickly its message will speak to your heart. The Bible is precious to our family, and we want you to have this one as a gift."

Trouble examined the Bible with a serious look of awe and gratitude.

"May I see it too, Trouble?" Carrie asked.

Trouble shared the Bible with her, and Mary moved her chair closer to the lounge. She turned to Trouble. "Perhaps you and Carrie will read it together. The Bible has wonderful stories I'm sure you both will like, but there is so much more. It's a book for all ages. We hope your parents will someday want to read it too."

Carrie smoothed the leather cover of the Scriptures. It felt good in her hands, as if it were meant to be there. "I've been thinking of church in regard to Trouble," she said. "He has a definite interest in it, and he has friends who ask if he reads the Bible. I think it embarrasses him to say no.

"Papa is against religion, so neither Trouble nor I have

read a Bible. Thank you for his gift." She turned to her brother. "You'll take excellent care of it, won't you?"

"Yes, I will," Trouble answered reverently. "You don't know how much I've wanted a Bible, Carrie. The Sanderson twins say it will change my life." Seeming enthralled, he headed for the back stairs to take the Bible to his room. Halfway to the stairs, he turned with a look back at the Nugents. "Please don't leave. I'll be right down."

A neighbor on horseback who stopped by the front gate delayed Mama and Papa in their return. Carrie, content to feast her eyes on Graham, waited for him to speak. His warm gaze never left her.

She wondered how her father could keep from comparing Graham Nugent with Alfred Rafter. What girl would not prefer Graham? So focused was Carrie on her thoughts that she realized she had missed a question from Mary.

"I beg your pardon. Would you repeat your question?"

"It was nothing, really," Mary said, then lowered her gaze. "I see your parents are coming in now."

The three smiled at the couple entering the room, and Gwendolyn turned to Cook, who followed. "I think we could all do with some more hot tea. We're both shivering from the cold air outside. As quickly as you can, please."

Mortimer kneaded his hands in front of the fireplace. "If you're shivering from cold, you should have come in. I could have talked to Farmer Jennings without your help."

Her father's reprimand humiliated Carrie, and she

longed to go to her mother and hold her. She tried to catch her eye, but Gwendolyn looked away. Carrie cast a pleading glance at their guests, and Mary Nugent rose quickly.

"Please don't bother with a tea tray, Mistress Warden. My husband, Riley, requested some time with Graham today, so we must get back. He's been unusually busy with his wood lathe and furniture business this week. It's only fair that he should have some time alone with Graham. We were all eager to learn if your daughter's health had improved, so Graham and I came as Riley's agents."

Cook left, and Gwendolyn, her hands visibly trembling, sat on a couch across the room from her guests. Twice she tried to speak, then finally made a request to Mary.

"I'm anxious about binding Carrie's injury, Mistress Nugent. I'm not certain I'm doing it correctly. Would you be so good as to spend a few minutes explaining how you bound it that first day?"

Mary Nugent picked up her reticule and moved to sit beside her hostess. Before they engaged in conversation, Carrie saw Mary touch Gwendolyn's hand lightly. She felt intense gratitude for her sensitivity to her mother.

Mortimer chose to ignore his wife's embarrassment. When Graham attempted to speak to Carrie, he interrupted rudely to occupy Graham's attention himself. Carrie knew he didn't care that his bad manners were so obvious.

"So you're reading law, are you?" he declared, settling in his padded lean-back chair. "All the lawyers I know are poor. Seems to me you could have chosen a more lucrative profession. What do you intend to do in the future?"

Again Carrie felt shame. Would the Nugents ever want to see them again? Would Graham want to see her again?

Graham leaned forward. "I'm ready to do whatever God wants me to, Sir. When I started reading law, I approached my uncle Frederick in Philadelphia. So far, it has worked out well. What happens now is up to the Lord. The Bible makes it clear that when we obey God, He directs our path. We can depend on it."

Carrie cringed at her father's disdainful smirk, but she was proud of Graham's forthright answer.

"I am not a church member, myself," Mortimer said. "The church has brought my family nothing but heartache. As far as the future, I depend on business for my security. What you invest with hard work comes back multiplied tenfold. Those with weaker hearts can depend on the church." He laughed scornfully. "I wish them luck."

Not deterred, Graham answered in a firm voice. "I consider hard work necessary too, but I make it a practice to serve the Lord through my church and my business. My days go better if I start them by talking to God."

Carrie listened, enjoying Graham's straightforward answers. She wished the two of them had time to talk alone. She'd like to know how he came to believe in

God. She wanted to know all about him, but there was no time. Papa had given her a week to settle her mind on Alfred Rafter; and though her accident had extended the date, the threat still loomed like a nightmare.

Up to now, Alfred Rafter's visits, replete with flattery and faultfinding, had brought nothing but headaches. She could barely abide being in the same room with the man more than five minutes at a time.

Why couldn't women have the same freedom men enjoyed? Rafter could secure his choice with a mere request. She had no choice. Trapped like an animal, she was forced to marry whomever her father wished.

It would be different if she were poor. Sometimes girls in town fell in love and married at sixteen or seventeen. Many girls her age had babies already. But those girls didn't have to marry men who would enhance their fathers' business prospects. Unlike her, they were free.

❧

Graham continued to converse with Mortimer Warden, while inside, fury ate at him. It was all he could do to keep smiling and ignore the insults both Carrie and her mother had received. Carrie's face expressed her mortification. The head of this family needed the Lord more than any mortal he had ever met.

He would have loved to present the Bible to the family instead of just to Trouble. Yet the likelihood of seeing Mortimer throw the Bible into the fire was more than he or his mother could endure.

He felt no guilt at giving Trouble the Bible without

Carrie's parents knowing. They had no right to keep God's Word from their children—all of them. Three families outside their home had no spiritual ties to Jesus because Mortimer Warden prejudiced them against the Savior. It could be that only through young Travis would his family come to the Lord.

What about Carrie? Her attitude grew softer each time they met. Graham believed God was preparing her heart for Christ's sweet entry, and he could hardly wait to see it happen. All things were possible with that eventuality.

❧

During the weeks of her recovery, Carrie was not pressed to set a date for her marriage. Graham and Mary called often to inquire after her health, once bringing a pair of fancy wooden crutches.

Gwendolyn's pale face recorded shock when she brought the couple into the parlor. "Um, Carrie, Dear, the Nugents have brought something Mr. Nugent made in his home woodshop." She wrung her hands and addressed Graham. "If you helped make these, I think we'd better wait until Mortimer gets home before we accept them." Carrie realized her mother failed to grasp how insulting her remark sounded.

Smiling, Graham laid the crutches, wrapped in a sheath of muslin, on the floor beside Carrie's lounge. "These are meant to give you some freedom, Carrie. Knowing how much you like the outdoors, Father thought that by using them you could walk in the yard again." He unfurled the muslin.

Carrie and Gwendolyn both gasped at the beauty of the polished, hand-carved crutches. "Oh, how lovely," Carrie exclaimed, stroking the shining wood. With a knowing look at Graham, she asked, "Did your father really make these for me?"

Mary spoke quickly, her gaze on Gwendolyn. "Not altogether. Graham did have a hand in making them. A big hand." She saw Graham's frown and addressed him. "Graham, I won't ignore your help just to spare Mr. Warden's feelings."

Gwendolyn's hand went to her cheek. "What? What do you mean? Tell me what you're talking about."

"I apologize, Mistress Warden, but I'm confused by the fact that you must have your husband's permission for our visits or to give Carrie a gift to help her walk again. I think it perfectly logical that we should want to follow her progress and help her recover. It's the main reason Graham and I have come so often to check on her. No one has sent word of her condition to us, and we were concerned."

Gwendolyn lowered her head. "I understand, but I'm not sure Mortimer does. He has a schedule of his own, and the family and I must be careful not to disturb him unduly."

Mary's mouth dropped open. "Riley has never limited my participation in family events, Mistress Warden. Nor has he restricted my personal opinions. I'm not certain what my reaction would be if he tried."

"Mortimer is very capable. He is a businessman who has proved his worth in heading up a large company and a large family. Wives must respect their husbands, he says. The man of the house has to be respected above all else."

"Respect is earned, Mistress Warden."

"This is no time to be critical, Mother," said Graham, placing an arm around his mother. "I'm sorry, Mistress Warden. You too, Carrie. Mother has seen how hard we've worked to get the crutches exactly right. We even talked to Dr. Winstock to make sure we balanced them correctly. She's disappointed."

Carrie's pride in Graham multiplied. *What a fine lawyer he must be!* A man of vision. Knowing that fact took away the sting of her own hurt feelings. Nevertheless, Mistress Nugent was right. Her mother had given her father's absurd demands her foremost consideration, disregarding the urgent needs of her family.

Mary Nugent was just plain tired of trying to follow Mortimer Warden's unreasonable rules in order to do something good. Carrie wondered what Mary would say if she knew he had promised her to a man as old as he was? She made a decision. Given the opportunity, she would tell Mary her sad story and ask her advice.

Gwendolyn accepted Mary's apology and helped Carrie, with Mary's assistance, to try the crutches. Graham stayed within arm's length in case he was needed.

"This is wonderful!" Carrie exclaimed, moving slowly with her good foot and the crutches. "I can actually walk again!"

"Don't take too many steps at first," Graham cautioned. "In fact, it might be better if you rest awhile now."

"No, you mustn't get too tired," Gwendolyn added.

Mary placed her hand on the other lady's shoulder. "If Mr. Warden objects to the crutches, I hope you will stand with Carrie and insist she be permitted to use them. You can see how weak she is when she tries to stand. The crutches will help her get her strength back."

Gwendolyn nodded. "I. . .I'm sure you're right." But her face held a different emotion.

That evening, when Carrie and her mother broached the subject of the crutches with Mortimer, the conversation went better than expected. He saw the need for her return to good health, Carrie supposed, for the good of the arrangement.

Carrie and Trouble read the Bible together nearly every night. It became the most vital part of their day, igniting discussions that lasted until bedtime.

The Nugents came a little less often; but when Gwendolyn and Mary were otherwise occupied, Carrie and Graham managed many precious moments together.

During one of their brief afternoons, Carrie asked Graham what made him love God as he did and how he had become so sure of what he believed.

That day a new relationship between Carrie and Graham began.

eleven

"Trouble and I have been reading the Bible together, and we have questions. You've helped us already, but we need your answers again. Do you mind?"

Graham's smile told her he welcomed the request. "I'm not the Bible scholar I want to be, but I'll help you insofar as I'm able. I expected you to have questions, and I hoped you'd let me discuss them with you."

Carrie folded a pillow under her arm to change her position on the lounge. "My first question is probably one you expected." She lowered her lashes and asked timidly, "Graham, have you always believed in God?"

His sincere look exposed deep feelings. "Yes, I have. My parents taught me simply by the way they believed. But I trusted Jesus with my life because I realized that faith in Him was the only truth that made sense. Not only does He control my life, Carrie, I believe He controls the entire world as well."

Carrie smiled. "Jesus seems a most wonderful person, but do you really believe He came to earth as a human and that He is actually the Son of God?"

"I do," he declared. "Carrie, perhaps I should have advised you and Trouble to start with one particular book of the Bible. It's the Book of John, and reading that will help you know my Savior better."

"Are the Ten Commandments in that book?"

"No, the commandments are found in the Old Testament. The Book of John is in the New Testament. The Old Testament gives the history of God's relationship with the Jews and prophecies about Jesus Christ. The New Testament is about His ministry on earth. John gives us a good deal of information about Jesus as the Son of God.

"For instance, John quotes Jesus Himself in chapter 14, verse 1, 'Let not your heart be troubled: ye believe in God, believe also in me.' Then, in verse 6, Jesus says, 'I am the way, the truth, and the life: no man cometh unto the Father, but by me.'"

"So that's why Jesus is so important."

"Yes. You and Trouble will discover many treasures in the Book of John. When you both come to know Jesus personally, the study of His Word will bring you more understanding and greater happiness."

Thinking of her unhappy future, Carrie clutched the arm of the chaise lounge. She respected Graham for his strong beliefs, but, faced with her current circumstances, what he felt gave her little comfort.

"That's a hard statement to accept," she said softly. "What if, in the scheme of things, happiness is not possible?"

"When we accept Jesus, God's Spirit comes to live in our hearts. Besides helping us make the right choices every day in our lives, He gives us courage and strength to endure anything the world hurls at us."

Though Graham's face radiated confidence, Carrie felt dismal inside. She had no confidence that simply accepting Jesus would change anything. Would she ever completely understand what Graham was talking about?

Her next question was a natural one. "How do you know this thing they call salvation really happens, Graham?"

"Because I've experienced it, and someday you and Trouble will experience it too." He sat back in his chair, not wanting to press her further. "Now, I think I'd better find Trouble and make sure he's present when your mother returns. It's fortunate your mother felt like walking out with my parents to show them the small pond. I've ridden by it. With the cedars and places to sit, you have quite a pleasant little park down there. Maybe you, Trouble, and I can picnic there someday."

Trouble slipped around the door to surprise them. "I was listening," he said, rubbing his nose and watching for a negative reaction. When none came, he said, "Mr. Nugent, you said some of the same things the Sanderson twins have told me." Voices of the parents filtered through the house from the back door. "I wish we had time to talk a little more, but I guess we shouldn't. Mama might—"

Carrie reached for his hand. "Perhaps later, Trouble. We'll work it out."

❧

Following another visit from the Nugents two days later,

Trouble left for the barn to feed Bandy and Samantha. Gwendolyn brought a basket of cotton strips, a towel, and a pan of warm water and soap to change the dressing on Carrie's ankle. Unwrapping the ankle, she exclaimed, "Look, Dear, this worst bruise is turning yellow. You're a healthy girl, and the healing is going well. I'm sure Mistress Nugent's expert care so soon after you were injured is the reason. Soon it will only be a memory."

Carrie smiled at her mother's optimism. She wiggled her foot and felt hardly any pain. "You're right. Maybe I can take a few steps when you get the bandage back on."

"I'm not sure your father would want you walking yet. He wants you absolutely well, and I'm sure you know the reason why," Gwendolyn said, reaching for the water and towel.

"Mama, please tell me I may try. You know the condition of my leg. You are the one who has tended it. Even with the crutches, I'm so immobile. I'm sorry my leg is still sore, but I'm so tired of this lounge, and embroidery, and needlepoint, and knitting, and. . .and sitting! Please, let me try to walk."

"Do take that scowl off your face, Carrie, and stop whining. Above all, please say 'my limb.' In this house, we should not use that indelicate word."

Carrie grimly watched her mother wash and dry her ankle and foot, then bind it with the clean cloth. Encouraged by how much better she felt, she wondered when she'd be able to ride again. She lay back, remembering the rolling fields, the cool air tingling her cheeks as it rushed by. Graham galloped silently into her daydream. Graham on Raven... A sigh escaped her lips, and her mother's gaze fixed steadily upon her.

Gwendolyn gathered up the basket and other items she had used and placed them on a table by the door. Turning, she moved to sit on the footstool again. "Carrie, I won't have you thinking I'm oblivious to what is happening. I know you and Trouble have arranged time alone for you and Graham Nugent, and you may be dreaming about something you hope will happen. But it changes nothing."

Her mother stared into her eyes. "Your father has made an agreement with Alfred Rafter that the two of you will be married. He has refrained from pressing the wedding arrangements because you were unwell. When you're able to walk, those plans will be finalized."

Tears rose in Carrie's eyes. Her afternoons with Graham had been magical. In the power of his blue-eyed attention, she had brushed aside thoughts of the arranged marriage and once again dared to hope. Why couldn't her parents see how mismatched she and Rafter were? Marriage to the man would be like a death sentence. Her rebellious heartbeat accelerated, and she could hardly breathe.

But Gwendolyn hammered the piercing truth still deeper. "I know you've hoped your father would relent, but you will be disappointed." She took a deep breath. "Mortimer is aware you are attracted to Graham Nugent, although he has no fortune other than a few acres of land on the bay and as his father's heir to the furniture business. The fact that he intends to practice law is another mark against him. Mortimer says he will be poor."

"But, Mama—"

"Listen to me! Can you imagine the limitations you would have to accept, married to a man with no money? You must put away your romantic ideas and follow the rich future your father has so generously provided."

Her mother rose and turned her back to Carrie. Seconds later she moved to a window and nipped dead leaves from a windowsill plant. Her fingers trembled. Carrie knew why. *It's because she's so unsure of herself. She wrings her hands only when she's very nervous.*

But her mother was not through. In a quavering voice, she said, "There's one thing more. Mistress Rafter has consented to help you learn the housekeeping schedule she follows. When you can walk, she will start you on simple duties, progressing to more complex tasks as you are able.

"The Rafters have a large home with many servants. Since you will be mistress of the house, the Rafters are eager for you to learn their routine so you will not be cheated or tricked by crafty servants or tradesmen. Mr. Rafter's home must be properly run. It is very generous of them to teach you."

Carrie faced sheer terror. It was all going too fast! Her parents had called forth a monster to devour her! What could she do? There must be some way to escape that dreadful prospect. Trouble had promised he would help her run away, and his way out now seemed the only possibility. Wiping a tear from her cheek, she made one last attempt to get through to her mother.

"Oh, Mama! Why can you never be on my side? You've agreed to let the Rafters treat your younger daughter like an indentured servant merely because they are wealthy! How could you?" Carrie's tears spilled over and streamed down her face as her mother headed for the door. "Mama," she cried, "come back and talk to me. Mama, please! I'm only nineteen!"

twelve

That night as Carrie lay in bed, she heard her parents in a rare argument. Papa's voice dominated the dispute, and tears slipped from Carrie's eyes in regret. She thought of the sweet harmony between the Nugents, and she wished, without meaning to demean her relatives, that she were a member of that family.

Now and then her mother's indistinct words came from below the stairs. Even from her room, Carrie recognized them as pleas. Why and what was she pleading? Was she sorry after all about Carrie's situation? Maybe her mother would. . .

She heard a sound at her door. It opened slowly, and Trouble tiptoed inside. He crept to her bed and peered into her face to see if she was awake.

"Yes, I heard them too," she said. "Get up on the bed, Trouble, and cover your feet so you won't catch cold."

Trouble did as she asked and settled down facing her, his legs crossed. "Papa wants you and Mama to plan your wedding with old Mr. Rafter, I'll bet. Isn't that what their quarrel is about?"

"I can't tell for sure, but I'm afraid you're right, Trouble."

Trouble slapped the covers. "It's not fair! You and Graham were starting to like each other. Pretty good too,

I think." He caught her hand. "Carrie, you're not going to let them make you marry old Mr. Rafter, are you? I don't want him for a brother-in-law."

"There's no way out of it, Trouble." Though ashamed her younger brother was witness to her fading confidence, she started to cry again.

"Oh, Sister, don't waste time crying!" he chided, wrapping the counterpane around his feet. "We have to plan your escape! Have you got any ideas yet?"

Carrie leaned over and kissed him. "You're such a dear to try to help me, Trouble. Everyone except you is pushing me into this marriage. You're the faithful one, the only one who's on my side."

Trouble patted her arm. "Have Mama and Papa told you about the invitation?"

Carrie wiped her eyes. "What invitation?"

"The Nugents sent an invitation today for us to come to their party for Mistress Nugent's birthday."

Carrie's heart began its familiar quick beat. "Trouble, is it true? You're not just saying that to make me feel better, are you?"

"No, it's true. I looked at the invitation when Mama went to the root cellar with Cook."

The edge of a full moon peeked through the window; Trouble's shadowy face told Carrie how earnest he was. "How did you find out about the invitation? Who delivered it?" she whispered.

"It wasn't Graham. I think it was a man who works for Mr. Nugent. The invitation said they were asking the whole family like they did before. Half the town is invited. Even the Rafters. I heard Mama and Papa talking about it."

Leaning forward, Carrie pulled up her knees and folded her hands on them as a chin rest. "That may be what the argument's about. Mama probably wants to go, and Papa won't say he'll go until he finds out if the Rafters intend to accept."

"If we get to go, it would give you a chance to see Graham. With all those people, no one would notice if you were together or not. It would be natural for you and Graham to talk."

She thought for a moment. "I wonder if Papa will let us go? What do you think, Trouble? I'm almost afraid to hope."

"Don't give up so easily. Mama may talk him into it. She admires Mistress Nugent. I guess it's because she spoke up that day when she was here. Mama never thought about Papa earning people's respect before."

Sighing, Carrie murmured, "I don't know, Trouble. Since it's the Nugents' celebration, there's not much chance Papa will consent. Mama says he knows all about the time Graham and I have spent together."

From below, raised voices intruded on their conversation.

"I'm going to slip out and listen!" Trouble was off the bed and out the door in seconds.

"Trouble, don't!" Carrie cautioned.

But the boy was gone. She waited anxiously as the minutes slipped by.

He bounced back on the bed in excitement. "Wait till you hear! I heard the whole thing. Mama said that since Mistress Nugent had been so nice to help you and they had visited and brought the crutches, flowers, and other gifts, it would be an insult to turn down another invitation. She told Papa it would be bad for his business not to go. I'm glad she thought of that! Papa heard her then," he said, finishing with a soft giggle.

"And what did Papa answer?" Carrie held her breath.

"He said he didn't know they had made so many visits. They had another argument then, and Mama cried a little. Then he said all right, we could go, but he intended to watch you like a hawk!"

Carrie clasped her hands to her heart. "Trouble, I don't know how to pray, but if there's even a chance that Graham's God listens to prayers, let's pray right now that nothing keeps us from going to the Nugents' party."

Together they bowed their heads, and Carrie prayed that she would have the chance to talk to Graham. If she did, she'd tell him how she and Trouble were continuing to read the Bible. She'd also say that though they were only beginners, they were starting to understand why Graham believed as he did.

Afterward, when Trouble went to his room, Carrie snuggled down in bed and listened to rain patter on the roof. Cozy and warm, she postponed her plan of escape and imagined the party at the Nugents', the opportunity she and Graham would have to talk, and the secret words they'd use to communicate their deepest thoughts.

❧

"Look your best tonight, Daughter. I believe Mr. Rafte
will have a surprise for you. This would be an exceller
time for any announcement he wishes to make."

Taking her time, Carrie stopped her father at the foo
of the long stairway. Deep in thought, he failed to notic
she was having trouble releasing her crutches to hang o
to the banister.

Mortimer continued. "At the same time, tonight wi
make perfectly clear to anyone else who has unfounde
ideas of attaching himself to you that you are not avail
able. Alfred Rafter is a rich man, and he will be riche
When you marry, he will be your choice. Now, let m
help you to your room."

Although she didn't know the right words, in despera
tion Carrie prayed to Graham's God. *No, no! Please don
let it be!*

Distracted by her father, Carrie misjudged the first ste
and stumbled against him. He hardly noticed. Dismall
she concentrated on getting up the stairs. Papa wasn
hefty enough to carry her as Graham had. She'd have t
manage on her own.

Using a crutch and the railing to negotiate the step:
she conquered the first half. Her father, stepping lightl
ahead, carried the second crutch. Her rebel self cleare
her mind of the present and envisioned the night ahea
at Graham's home.

She would wear the prettiest gown she owned. Mad
of golden damask, the shining fabric caressed her nec

and shoulders with its warmth and complemented her red-gold hair. Piled high by the maid, Carrie's hair would lie in delicate swirls, entwined with a narrow velvet ribbon to match her dress.

With the dress, she would wear her amber necklace and eardrops, a gift from Papa. Purchased to impress Alfred Rafter, Papa's gift had not impressed Carrie until she tried them with the golden dress. She thought of Graham and his first view of her, and her mouth lifted in a smile. Fortunately, Papa misread her thoughts.

"Daughter, I believe you are thinking of the amusement you and Trouble will enjoy at the party tonight. I warn you, do not call attention to yourself.

"Of course, you must offer polite birthday greetings to Mistress Warden, but then I insist you stand by the Rafters and make sure they receive the honor due them. They deserve our utmost respect for responding to an invitation that is far beneath their social status. I think the fact that they consented to attend speaks of greatness on their account."

They had reached Carrie's room, and her father helped her inside.

"All right, there you are," he said, seeming relieved to finish his task. "I will send the girl up to help you, but I reiterate: You are to be wholly attentive to Alfred Rafter and his family. They expect you to stay close to them, and I shall be very angry if you do not. We have spoken together about the evening, and I assured them of the pleasure of your company the entire time."

Without another word, he turned abruptly and left the room. Carrie scooted back and rested against the stacked pillows on her bed to catch her breath. Papa had warned her, so she must not avoid the Rafters.

But she would be in the Nugent house! She could admire Graham, and it would be impolite not to speak with him at all. Other opportunities were sure to present themselves. The Nugents would see to her comfort, which might also involve him. Anything was possible.

Her mind reviewed the days they had been together. Their stolen hours had taught her much about his character. He was a gentle man and sensitive to the feelings of others. She especially remembered the day Trouble had delved deeper into Graham's relationship with God. They had walked down the hall to the big living room so Carrie could practice her balance on the new crutches.

Graham had put his arm around the boy. "As I told Carrie, Trouble, in my case building a relationship with the Lord wasn't hard to do. My mother and father always studied the Bible with me. The Bible was my first reader. But reading it did not make me a Christian. I had to believe what the Bible said."

At their destination, Carrie sat on a couch and rested her leg on a stool.

Graham paced the rug in front of the fireplace as if infused with energy by his favorite subject. Intrigued, Trouble glanced at Carrie. "Go ahead, Mr. Nugent. Tell us more," he said, taking a seat beside her.

"In those days, we lived in New York. When I went to

Philadelphia to read law with Uncle Frederick, my parents bought property and moved here for business reasons." He glanced at Carrie uneasily. "I'm sorry to say they've made friends with everyone in the area except your parents."

Carrie knew why. Categorizing the Nugents as church people, her parents would have wanted nothing to do with them. "It wasn't your parents' fault, Graham," she replied.

"I think you were really lucky to have parents who wanted you to read the Bible," Trouble said.

"Not lucky, Trouble, blessed. I started to notice how people who truly loved the Lord were different from the rest. I admired them. They were like those I'd read about in the Bible. They were like Jesus. They had made Him Lord of their lives."

In their private study, Carrie and Trouble had drawn from the Old Testament the prophecies about Jesus. The story of His life, recounted in the Gospels, they found even more fascinating. As if to affirm what they had learned, here was Graham, talking about how those inspired words had personally reached his heart.

"Each of those people I grew to admire told the same story," Graham continued. "Individually, they had come to a point where they understood why Jesus came in human form. People could relate their daily lives to Him. For their sins, God had sent His perfect Son, Jesus, to die on a cross for them.

"I began to comprehend the fact that Jesus died for

me too, and I asked myself why. The answer was simple. He loved me with a love too great to imagine. In front of the believers who gathered in our house one night, I asked Jesus to come into my heart."

Resting on her bed before dressing for the party, Carrie felt her heart beat strangely. It was the same way she'd felt that day when Graham told the story of his salvation. Since then, Trouble too had seemed quieter than usual, sometimes lost in thought when spoken to.

Carrie moved her leg to a more comfortable position and tried to reason out her anxiety. She decided what she felt was simply fear of what would come next. Somehow, asking Jesus into her heart seemed like stepping into a vast unknown.

She stopped, stunned by an idea. *Is that what the Bible means by "faith"? Does every person have to take that step? Alone? Is that what God wants?* She raised herself on her elbows and wished for Trouble. And Graham. Her heart pounding wildly, she felt as if she had just made a remarkable discovery!

thirteen

Music flowed into the night from the Nugent house, alight with dozens of candles. Attached to the overhang of the front porch, lanterns lit the path for the Wardens, arriving in their covered carriage.

At least ten carriages and buggies sat in the moonlight along the front drive, and in a lot on the leeward side of the home, twice as many horses stamped and nickered, tended by a young man Carrie recognized as the blacksmith's apprentice. Breathlessly, she waited for Papa to descend from the carriage and help her mother down.

The Nugent house was not as large as the Wardens', but Carrie thought it far more welcoming than their own mansion of stone. Constructed of white clapboard with neat green shutters, the home's charm was partly defined by whitewashed stones outlining beds cultivated for spring flowers. Inside a white picket fence, a wide flagstone path led between tall trees to the porch steps. Clusters of winter shrubs thrived at intervals around the foundation.

The whole did not compare in expense to the Warden house, yet the appearance of the neat, winsome dwelling tugged at Carrie's heart.

For this night, Carrie had left her crutches at home so as not to attract attention. Papa loaned her a mahogany walking stick with a silver inlaid handle. He thought it particularly stylish. While not as helpful as her crutches, the cane made walking on level ground rather simple.

Their man drove the carriage to the side of the house as Papa took the lead up the path. Her hand on Trouble's shoulder, Carrie managed the flagstone path with almost no pain. Before Papa could knock, Graham swung open the front door.

His handsome presence, in black trousers and jacket with a red vest and black leather boots, electrified the air. "Our warmest welcome to the Warden family! Come in, please. Come in!"

Carrie felt his gaze upon her as she stepped forward, and the emotions engulfing her were not the excitement of a birthday party. They had not seen each other for several days, and Graham's eyes revealed a similar exhilaration.

To see if the Rafters had arrived, Papa hurried to survey the crowd in the large main room. Poor Mama got the worst of it. As usual, he paid no attention to her comfort or dignity and ended up almost dragging her.

"May we take your coats and hats, Mr. Warden?" asked Graham, stepping up behind him. He tried to help Carrie off with her blue velvet winter cape.

"Never mind, Mr. Nugent. I'll attend to my daughter's wraps!" Papa ordered, bristling. "You just help my wife with hers. As son of the host of tonight's celebration, that's your only responsibility."

Amiably, Graham turned and smiled at Carrie's mother. "Of course. May I assist you, Mistress Warden?"

Her father passed Carrie's cape and scarf to a maid standing to one side. Carrie, striving to gain control of her emotions at the sight of Graham's striking appearance, relaxed and enjoyed the moment. His black hair neatly brushed back, his rugged face freshly shaved, and his dark brows and lashes accenting those astounding blue eyes, Graham was irresistible.

Yet she knew beneath that handsome countenance breathed a man of integrity and depth. On every occasion, he had proved himself a man whom she could depend upon to make the right choices. God controlled his life, he'd said, and he gave of himself without thought of recompense. Those qualities made the difference between Graham and other men she knew.

Alfred Rafter certainly was not a godly man. He was as much against religion as her father. Once she married him, there would be no Bible reading, and she and Trouble would probably lose touch in religious matters. At least Trouble would likely stay in close communication with the Nugents. Carrie would have no one to advise her spiritually.

With Graham, she had opened her heart to a remembered promise. He was the "romantic man" Grandmother Lawrence cautioned her to wait for, and his faith possessed the depth of her grandfather's. Graham won the key to her heart because he was a believer too.

Though at odds when they first met, she admitted now that she had known from that moment he was the one she'd waited for.

Judging from her fascinated stare, Graham's appearance stunned Gwendolyn as well, for when Papa walked back and tried to get her attention, he had to speak twice. "Gwendolyn," he said, still craning to look for the Rafters. "Gwendolyn! Did you hear me? Come along!"

Nearly stepping on the maid's toes, he grabbed Carrie's free arm and, glaring at Graham, pushed her ahead of them. Graham followed with Trouble, who had dressed in his best black suit for this special party.

"You put up decorations!" he exclaimed over the noise and the music of a string trio in the parlor.

"By all means, Trouble. We knew you were coming. There are more decorations inside." He caught Carrie's eye and said directly to her, "We wanted everything beautiful for you."

Mary and Riley Nugent came from the parlor door. With her wonderful smile, Mary greeted them. "Good evening, Mr. and Mistress Warden! Hello to you too, Carrie and Travis! How lovely to have you all in our home. I hope your other children will honor us with their presence. We're looking forward to knowing them better."

"Well, I'm not sure they'll be here," Gwendolyn stammered. "You know how grown children are. They may have family plans of their own. But Letitia wanted to come, so she and Joshua may try to venture out."

"They may not, however," Mortimer snapped, his mouth a thin line. "Joshua had extra work to finish at the mill."

Carrie searched her father's face for sincerity and frowned. Did he give Joshua extra work to keep him from coming to the Nugent party? She remembered Letitia's disappointment at not being able to accept the Nugents' Christmas Eve invitation and hoped this would not be a repeat.

"Indeed!" added Riley, shaking Mortimer's hand. "Children do have minds of their own, as they should have. But let's get on to the festivities! We have long awaited a visit from you four. We're grateful you've come to celebrate my beautiful wife's birthday."

"Thank you," Mortimer said, still searching the crowded room for the Rafters. Carrie held her breath and looked too. "I see the Rafters have not arrived yet," he said. "I expected them to be here by now."

"Oh?" Riley said. "Well, they were probably delayed and will arrive presently. Shall we join the others? Greet your friends and have some tidbits to eat. Let the maids help you to some hot drinks."

Mortimer took Gwendolyn's arm, sheathed in the lace of her navy gown. Seeming momentarily at ease, he allowed the Nugents to lead them on a tour through the house, introducing them to townspeople Carrie knew they were not friendly with under ordinary circumstances. She and Trouble turned back to talk to Graham.

Making the most of unexpected time alone, Graham whispered to Trouble and pointed toward a cluster of youngsters his own age in the parlor. Trouble left to join them, and Graham grabbed Carrie's arm.

"Follow me. No arguments!"

He gently led her to the front of the house, and they slipped inside his father's study. Shutting the door, he turned, swept her a look from head to toe, and reached for her. Lifting her off the floor in a tender embrace, his eager lips covered hers in a long kiss. Breathless, she clung to him because she could not have stood by herself.

Holding her close, he whispered, "I promised my- self the last time I left you that if I ever again had the opportunity to kiss you, I would grab it. I have no apology to make."

"Nor do I ask for one."

Holding her face between his hands, he caressed her cheek with his thumb. "Carrie, tell me. . .please tell me you feel the same affection for me that I feel for you."

She kissed his hand, her brown eyes answering the plea in his. "You know I do."

"Then we have to find a way out of this trap you're in. If we can—"

"Graham, do you know about the trap I'm in? I mean, the whole ugly story and the fact that Papa is practically selling me to Rafter for better business prospects? It's all so awful."

Feeling her face flush with embarrassment, Carrie leaned her forehead against his chest. She hadn't dreamed he knew all the repulsive details of the arrangement.

Graham raised her chin and drew her close. "Suffice it to say that God Himself may have brought us together. I prefer to think He did. Only He could have selected a lady so right for me." He kissed her again.

Carrie caressed his cheek with her palm. "Soon everyone will know I'm to marry a man I can hardly stand so Papa can improve his business connections." A tear trailed down her cheek.

"Please don't cry, Carrie. We have to think this out and decide how to handle it. Our greatest obstacle is your father's dislike of me and my family."

"Oh, Graham, how awful. Are your parents aware of the way my parents feel? They've been so wonderful to me. I love them. I couldn't stand it if they were hurt."

"I think they can bear up under your father's dislike. It's really only me who's the threat. He fears that we feel about each other exactly as we do. You and I have to find a way to win him over. In the meantime, we must stop the wedding arrangements." He smiled broadly. "Do you think you could sprain the other ankle? That seems safest. I don't believe in duels."

"Graham, do be sensible," she said, her sadness turning to a giggle. "What shall we do?"

A knock sounded at the door, and they sprang apart. The knock came again, louder.

"Yes?" Graham answered soberly.

"Graham, it's your mother. Come out quickly, or let me come inside."

Graham opened the door in haste. "What is it?" he asked as she slipped through the door.

Mary Nugent gave him an anguished look. "What do you suppose, Graham? Carrie's father is frantic. I can see with my own eyes what has transpired here, but you've placed Carrie in a very compromising position, Son. What possible excuse can you have?"

"I don't have one, Mother, and because you are the one person who might understand, I must be truthful. When I saw this golden girl looking so beautiful, I thought I would surely die if I didn't kiss her at once. So I did. You have no idea how long I've resisted." Graham chuckled, though the eyes gazing into Carrie's were serious.

"We've had no time to think out our problems yet, Mother, so we have no explanation. The obstacles we must overcome will mean a change for everyone Carrie knows. If we had just a few minutes more to talk, we might be able to think of something. Couldn't you go out and make our excuses?"

"You mischievous spirit! As if I were not party enough to your schemes already," Mary moaned. "Every time you wanted to see her, I accompanied you!"

"I'm sorry, Mistress Nugent. It's my fault. I wanted to see Graham too." Carrie turned to him with a long look. "More than anything."

"I had to be with her, Mother. You know that. But we're dealing with the present now. We love each other, and one mammoth problem must be solved before anything positive can result."

Mary's smile was interrupted by another knock at the door. This time Trouble appeared. "So there you are! I was sent to find you, Carrie. The Rafters are here, and Papa is searching everywhere for you. He'll be in here soon."

He looked around the study and frowned. "What are you doing in here anyway? Talking?" The other three exploded with laughter, and Trouble defended himself. "I only came to warn you, that's all."

"We're not laughing at you, Trouble." Graham placed a placating hand on the boy's shoulder. "This is about something completely unrelated to your appearance. Thank you for your warning. Now, let's all straighten our faces and go into the party together so no one else will become curious and look for us."

Graham opened the door, and they filed out into the crowd.

fourteen

While the knowledge that Graham loved her remained in her heart, Carrie dreaded with each step the first glimpse of her father's angry face. She wished she had asked Graham to pray for her. She put a bright smile on her face and raised her chin to converse with Mary.

"The house looks beautiful, Mistress Nugent. You've used winter apples and pinecones to create a lovely backdrop for the candles, and I see you've lit so many. Every room is bright and beautiful," she gushed, trying to cover her frustration.

"Wait until you see the table!" Trouble said. "It's loaded with all kinds of food. Meat and dumplings and candied apples and hot biscuits and I don't know what all. And on a table against the wall are pies and cakes and tarts and cookies and—"

"I think you've given us a clear picture of the food, Trouble," Carrie interrupted with a laugh.

Smiling, Graham greeted men in the crowd, but Carrie dared not direct a word of conversation to him. Papa would react loudly and violently and make her regret it if he saw. Yet Graham was there. If she liked, she could reach out and touch him; once in awhile, ever so covertly, he did touch her. His touch strengthened her, and she glided proudly through the room in her golden dress.

At that moment her father's eye caught hers, and he made a beeline across the room. Carrie felt as if she had lost the power to breathe. Rudely ignoring the others, Papa fastened a grip on her arm.

"Come with me! The Rafters are here, and Alfred is eager to speak to the crowd with you beside him."

Fearing what lay ahead, Carrie pulled back instinctively. Graham stepped forward, but, knowing his interference would gain nothing, she shook her head slightly and followed her father.

At a point in the center of the room, Mortimer presented Carrie before Rafter. She could not make herself meet the man's gaze. Behind him, Mistress Rafter and Ermagene stood with sour faces, obviously at odds with what was about to happen.

Taking the arm her father had loosed, Rafter turned her toward the people, who backed away to allow space for them. Carrie watched Graham's face register suspicion, then fury. She warned him with a frown. As much as she'd prefer it, a confrontation could cause dire consequences. The two businessmen might be prepared to ruin Graham's reputation. Just now, rescue was impossible; survival became her only goal.

Mortimer stepped forward. "Friends and neighbors, I have a delightful task, one I have long waited to bring to fruition. Tonight, I am happy to announce the coming marriage of my daughter, Carrie, to Mr. Alfred Rafter."

A wave of murmurs swept the room.

"My wife and I are proud of this honor granted ou daughter, and we wish to thank Mr. Rafter for his gen erosity to our family in selecting her. We intend Carrie' wedding to be the outstanding event of the summe season. Those who wish to attend are invited to ou home for the nuptial celebration. Thank you, and than you again, Mr. Rafter."

Carrie closed her eyes against the shame filling he heart. Papa was practically groveling before Alfred Rafter The crowd silenced except for murmurs of surprise an sympathy, which were loud enough for Carrie to hear She saw shock on the faces of people who knew her.

Minutes passed, with Rafter and her father makin; further remarks that offended Carrie. She wished th floor would collapse beneath her. Her face burned. N one congratulated them. No one talked.

Graham's face registered angry disbelief. She imag ined him caught between letting his anger consume hin and letting his God contain him. For Carrie, the realiza tion that they were in this together lessened the terror o being singled out. Tears started in her eyes, and sh blinked the them away.

Trouble sidled up to Graham and took his hand whil Mary Nugent deliberately moved behind a group of ta guests and watched the scene in tears. Only Rafter an Papa smiled. Then came a second humiliation.

Alfred Rafter held up his hands. "Quiet, please, quiet! No one had spoken, so Carrie failed to see any point t his loud command. He began again. "I'd like to seal our announcement with a gift for my future bride." He took a black cloth envelope from his vest pocket. "This is a ring my father gave my dear mother many years ago. Carrie, please hold out your hand."

Carrie couldn't move. When she didn't offer, he raised her hand and slid the ring on her finger. Large and ugly, the ring repelled Carrie. Graham turned away.

Much too large for her tiny hand, the ring dropped to the floor when Rafter let go of her hand. With an oath, he retrieved his gift and put it in his pocket. "I'll keep this for you until it's appropriate to give it to you again," he hissed in her ear.

Everyone seemed ashamed for her. Carrie wished she were dead. No! Not without Jesus. She was stunned by her own shocking truth. Her gaze swept the room, searching for Graham, but she could not find him.

Earlier, during their moment alone, she had desperately wanted to talk to him about her discovery of faith. Instead, she'd kissed him and passed up the opportunity.

Yet his kiss confirmed what she had known for months. Graham was the one. No one else would ever receive the little gold key to her heart. Sadly, their relationship had ended almost before it started. The key representing their love would be only a token of remembrance, taken out and touched now and then.

It seemed eerie that no one pressed forward to talk to her or Rafter. In fact, people were drifting away. Carrie was glad. The evening had turned into a nightmare.

Only her sister, Virgie, whom she had not noticed in the room before, moved close to give her a hug.

"Give yourself time," she whispered, but real regret shaded Virgie's eyes. Another wave of shock passed through Carrie. Had Virgie realized, at last, that Carrie's arranged marriage would be a mistake?

Carrie hadn't spoken to her other two female relatives since they arrived, nor to her brothers. They stood together in one corner of the room, talking to each other with lowered heads, not making eye contact. Her sisters-in-law, dabbing at their eyes with handkerchiefs, seemed to understand the pain she felt. And they weren't the only ones. Though girls her own age eyed her with sympathy and dismay, not one had the courage to speak.

Carrie wanted to apologize to the Nugents. After all their preparations, the hateful engagement announcement had turned the party into a disaster. Guests near her tried to make conversation by saying the right things. Yet more than once Carrie heard whispers of ". . .and she's so young," or "such an old man," until she felt nauseous. She moved about aimlessly, for no one seemed to want to approach her. Graham could not even try.

She moved away from her father and Rafter without their noticing. Strolling alone through the Nugent house, she was taken again by its loveliness. Original furniture built by Riley Nugent's company lent an air of polished perfection to each room. The inherent welcome of the home affirmed that Mary's first thought was for her family's comfort.

As she thought of that lady, Riley Nugent pushed through the crowd with a rolling table holding a towering birthday cake. Only a few candles dignified the cake, and Riley jovially advised the company of the reason.

"I wish all within the sound of my voice to know that if I'd had the baker set the correct number of candles on the cake, my Mary would chase me out of the house with her broom!" He chuckled and led his wife forward to blow out the candles.

Mary laughed heartily. "He's right about my chasing him out of the house with my broom. I've worn out five brooms that way! The problem is—he never learns!"

The crowd laughed, and for the first time since the announcement, the company seemed to relax. Minutes later the buffet was announced, and Riley asked for quiet. He spoke a blessing over the food, thanking God and giving Him the glory for all good gifts.

Supper found her father in charge of her table, which included the Rafters. Though the entrees would tempt most palates, Carrie barely looked at the display. Hoping her hostess didn't see, Carrie pushed food around her plate with her fork, but her heart was breaking, and she could not force herself to eat.

"My, my, it seems my little fiancée is not well," Alfred Rafter stated loudly. "She isn't partaking of her host's delicious repast." Looking at Mortimer, he added, "We must encourage her. We can't have our future new family member turn into a weakling, unable to carry her part of the load."

Diners at the surrounding tables went silent. Carrie felt her face flush. She hoped her father would say nothing, but at Rafter's words, he rebuked her.

"You're right, Alfred. She's not eating." Frowning across the table at Carrie, he chided in a callous voice, "Eat, Daughter! Do as Alfred says!"

Carrie glanced at her father, then cast her gaze above his shoulder. There she focused on a face so beloved the rest of the room faded. Graham stood near a bookcase that lay in a slight shadow. She felt enveloped by his love. He signaled with a nod of his head toward the back of the house, and Carrie said *yes* with her eyes.

❧

After supper she found the exact moment to slip away in silence to the back door. Lifting the latch, she stepped quickly outside. A heavy, warm coat closed around her shoulders, and she was pulled against a tall, firm body. Graham turned her to face him.

"You're here. My precious girl." He lifted her chin for his kiss.

Carrie clung to him, not wanting to let go. "Graham, I had no idea," she whispered.

"I know, Darling. They caught us off guard," he said, kissing her again. He cupped her face with his hands. "You're not to worry. God will show us a way. He's already there."

"Oh, I hope you're right."

"Believe me, He will." He kissed her cheeks. "You're cold. You must go in, but be calm, Carrie. Just wait. We must wait until everything is right. Will you promise me to wait without arguing with your father?"

"Yes," she said. "I've had a lifetime of waiting. I promised my grandmother I'd wait for you."

Graham chuckled. "I'll have to wait to hear that story. Now go quickly before they miss you."

Taking the coat from her shoulders, he pointed her toward the door, and she stole inside.

Graham was back in the house by the time the Rafters decided to leave. Mistress Rafter, dressed in her ostentatious widow's weeds, had a final maxim for Carrie.

"You must take advantage of what I'm about to tell you, Miss Warden. I know a great deal about the kind of wife my son needs. First of all, you must supplement your current meals with more meat, especially pork, and add ample portions of milk and butter. You're too small, and you need to gain weight and develop a firmer frame like our Ermagene."

"Listen to Mother, Miss Warden," Rafter agreed. "She will guide you as you attain the position of lady of the house. In fact, from now until we are married, she will be available to advise you. After our marriage she will instruct you in carrying out the schedule she has organized. You're very lucky she has decided to assist you."

Carrie's gaze found Graham, and she maintained a subdued countenance and said nothing. If no other escape opened, she would leave home. She was determined not to give in. A future as a member of the

Rafter family was unthinkable.

☙

Graham saw the quick shake of his mother's head and realized he must be frowning. Who wouldn't?

The pompous windbag! It was all Graham could do to keep from thrashing Alfred Rafter. Carrie did honor to his parents' home by remaining beautiful and serene. He knew, from his own anger, what it had taken for her to withstand the Rafters' harsh expectations of her.

Well, it was not to be. If he had to kidnap her from her home, he would not let Alfred Rafter marry his precious Carrie. She was calm, waiting for the next humiliation in front of their guests, and he had never loved her more. Shining like a sunbeam in her golden dress, her head high, and confident that he would somehow find a way to help her, she transmitted her love with a single, private glance at him.

The ire in Graham's heart diminished, and he knew he had done wrong.

Father in heaven, help us. Forgive me for these thoughts, and renew a right spirit within me. In my foolishness, I have ignored Your will and gone ahead of You. Of course, I must wait. You have the perfect plan for Carrie's happiness and for mine. Our plans mean nothing if You are not the author of them.

Up to now it seemed so right for us to be together. Yet, despite the fact that I want Carrie for my own, I will remain open to any change You wish to bring about in my mind. I beg You to forgive me for thinking only of my way instead of

Yours, and I pray I will be the servant You want me to be.
Thank You, Father. In Your blessed Son's name. Amen.

ஐ

The Rafters took their leave, and Papa, with no other
reason to stay, commanded his family to gather their
wraps for departure.

"Oh, please stay, Mr. Warden," Mistress Nugent
begged. "We still have a big pot of coffee and lots of
birthday cake left. Won't you linger and enjoy them,
sharing the rest of the evening with our guests?"

"No!" Mortimer snapped. "It's time to go." He offered
no more.

At Papa's urging, the family donned their heavy wraps
and proceeded to the door. The Nugents followed.

"It was lovely having you here for my birthday," Mary
said. "Please, come back anytime you will. You're always
welcome in our home. Good night, Carrie and Travis!"

Riley stuck out his hand to test the weather. "No
falling weather due, so they tell me. A clear night. That
will make for a fine ride home."

"May I help you walk Carrie out, Mr. Warden?"
Graham held out his hand to her. "She may need a hand
up to step into the carriage."

"No!" Mortimer barked. "That will not be necessary,
thank you."

Riley stepped forward. "Then please allow me, Miss
Warden," he said, taking Carrie's arm and walking
slowly with her as she pegged her way down the path.
He opened the gate wide so she and her cane could pass

through easily. "Mind the branch that's fallen from the tree. We wouldn't want you to fall again, would we?"

Carrie could imagine the look on Papa's red face, knowing he'd failed to manipulate the outcome after all. It had been the worst night of Carrie's life, but she could not leave without thanking Mr. Nugent for the family's invitation to the birthday party.

Her smile repeated itself in her eyes. "You have a wonderful home, Mr. Nugent. God has truly blessed you. Thank you for sharing it with us."

Riley's look darted to Graham, watching from the porch, and back to Carrie. "You're quite welcome, Miss Warden. I want you to know it's been gratifying having you here, getting to know you better." He helped her into the carriage, then passed her cane up to her.

Trouble came bounding up. "Good night, Sir. I had a good time tonight. I like Graham. He told me I could call him that. We're friends."

"I'm glad, Travis. I think Graham likes you—" He gave her a sly glance. "—and Carrie too."

Trouble looked over his shoulder at his father, then leaned toward Mr. Nugent. "Yes, but I think he likes Carrie in a different way."

Riley Nugent grinned widely and winked at her.

fifteen

In the carriage on the way home, Carrie tried to close her ears against the drone of Papa's tiresome comments about the Rafters. One man held her thoughts, and it was not Alfred Rafter.

"Mark my words, Carrie, one day you'll appreciate what I've done for you. You will never have to worry about money as long as you live. Eventually I believe you will be known in society as the matriarch of one of Maryland's most esteemed families. Have you thought of that?"

Carrie's answer came forth dully. "No, Sir."

Even her truthful reply irritated Mortimer. "Then I suggest you give it serious thought!" he shouted, alarming the two other drowsy passengers.

Regardless of his endless platitudes, only memories of Graham's kisses occupied Carrie's mind. Until tonight she had not let herself believe how much she loved him, for she was not positive he felt the same. Now she knew. Their time together had revealed all she needed to know, and her grandmother's promise had come true. Graham had turned an invisible key, opening her heart to him; and regardless of what happened, she would love him forever.

❧

In his room that night, Graham hung up his clothes and, almost in a trance, changed into his nightclothes. He had held his golden girl in his arms! *Carrie, Carrie, Carrie*—his heart sang her name.

How he loved her! And she loved him. He was sure of that now. Had she not confessed her feelings openly, he still would have known. Their proximity in a room sparked like lightning. The thrill of the sensation tingled within him.

Despite the resolve to wait on His will, Graham wondered how God would return her to his arms. He had to hope. His love for her overwhelmed him. If their future was meant to be, the Lord would make it perfect. Surely He would not let their affection progress this far, then allow her to marry Alfred Rafter.

It was possible God meant them to be together. Once Carrie became a Christian, and she would, the Savior would show them the way. She had an independent spirit, but a domineering father had nearly squelched her free will to choose God's plan for her life. Graham desired to help her independence reemerge in a positive way.

He had slipped a note to Trouble as the Wardens were leaving the party. The right response would prove the depth of Carrie's love for him. Though they had known each other for only a short time, tonight's confessions had planted a renewed confidence in Graham. God wanted his obedience. If he waited, if he was obedient and patient, the Lord would give him his heart's desire: Carrie.

Trouble made another of his bedtime visits to take Graham's note to his sister. Although awake, she had already gone to bed.

"What is it, Trouble? Did you come to see how unhappy I am?"

"Here! You must light a candle. Graham has written you a note." He handed her the paper.

Quickly Carrie sat up, lit a candle, and read the note aloud. "Carrie, I must talk to you. Ride out the first morning you can. I will watch for you. Please. Graham."

Collapsing against the pillows, she cried, "How can I, Trouble? I either have to use crutches or a cane to walk." She swiped at her eyes. "Can you imagine me clumping through the silent house like an elephant? It's impossible, and you know it! Graham hasn't thought of the obstacles. How could I ever manage to get into the saddle?"

"I can help you," Trouble said. "Just tell me what you want me to do. First, I can saddle Samantha and Bandy." Eager to be part of the plot, Trouble's eyes shone like candles reflected in a looking glass.

Carrie covered her face with her hands. Graham didn't realize the impossible thing he'd asked her to do. The servants would hear. Papa would. . .

Then she remembered the meaning of faith that she'd found on her own. Maybe it wasn't impossible. Maybe she should try. Graham must have thought of a plan to save her from marriage to Rafter. She could do it. She could pad her crutches so they would be soundless. And Trouble would help. She had to go!

"I'd like to try tomorrow," she said. "Can you get up early and be very, very quiet? If Papa should get wind of this, he'd lock me in my room until the wedding date with Rafter."

"Don't worry. I'll be quiet as a shadow. Be sure to dress warm, and I will too." He patted her hand in a fatherly way. "Just leave it to me, Carrie. I'll see you through."

He left then, looking as if he had settled everything and was very much in charge. Carrie lay back with a grin. What would she do without him?

❧

Carrie and Trouble slipped out of the house at dawn without waking any of the servants. In the barn, they used a feed trough as a launching place, and with Trouble's help, Carrie got onto Samantha's back. They kept their voices to a whisper.

"Are you balanced all right, Carrie? Make sure. We can't have you falling. We'd never be able to explain that," Trouble cautioned in a wispy voice.

"I'm fine, Trouble," she whispered. "Let's get out of here before someone discovers us and we have to go back in."

As soon as they were out of earshot, they cantered to a spot where they would be able to see Graham coming from any direction. He was nowhere in sight.

Panic hit Carrie. "He's not coming! Oh, I knew it. This

is going to get us into more trouble. We shouldn't have come. Let's go back before they find out we're gone!"

"Be calm, Sister. Give him a chance. He may have been delayed. Let's wait awhile. He'll be here."

After several minutes' wait, Carrie complained again. "Trouble, let's ride toward the crossroads. If we don't see him then, we'll have to go home. Something must have happened to keep him from coming, and we don't dare stay out until breakfast."

"All right," Trouble agreed, his voice remorseful.

They headed for the crossroads. No farther than a mile up the road, Graham came galloping toward them on Raven.

Trouble waved at him and looked up at Carrie. "I don't suppose you need me anymore, do you?"

Carrie was not sure. The closer Graham rode, the more anxious she became. "No, Trouble, don't leave yet. Stay with me for awhile. You may be in on this."

Graham pulled up beside them, looking so handsome Carrie did not remember to breathe. His eyes were magnetic. "Good morning. Both of you."

Carrie and Trouble responded with smiles, but Carrie was too nervous to remain out in the open for long.

"Graham," she said, "why don't we ride to that stand of cedars out by our little pond? We can talk there."

With a nod, Graham led off, and they trotted their horses down to the trees surrounding the pond. Graham slid from his horse; and while Trouble got off Bandy, he reached up to lift Carrie gently from Samantha's back.

He carried her to the bank of the pond. Fishermen had fashioned a bench of logs, and he placed her upon it.

"Are you comfortable?" he asked, capturing her gaze. She nodded, and he silently examined her face.

Unaware he'd interrupted a romantic moment, Trouble approached after tying up the horses. "While we're resting, could I ask you a question, Graham?"

"Sure, Trouble. Ask anything you want," Graham said.

"I want to know how Carrie and I can give our hearts to Jesus."

Graham glanced at Carrie as if she might protest, but she was equally eager for the answer. He stood, and Trouble sat beside Carrie. "In Romans 3:23, the Bible says everyone has sinned and fallen short of God's glory. In simple language, that means we all do bad things that deserve punishment. But because God loves us so much, He sent Jesus as a substitute to pay for our sins.

"Christ was perfect, yet He took all our sins upon Himself. He freely gave His life so we might be forgiven. When we accept the truth of what He did for us, His Holy Spirit lives in us until we meet Christ in heaven."

Carrie clutched her black cape close for warmth. "So if we believe that Jesus lived and is the Son of God who died for us, that's all He requires for the 'eternal life' you've spoken of?"

"Yes, but that's only the beginning. My desire is to see you two grow in the Lord through prayer and Bible study and service to God for the rest of your lives.

People call it the abundant life, and to true believers it's the only real happiness here on earth."

"Graham," Trouble said, "I want Jesus to come into my heart."

"So do I," Carrie added.

Looking from one to the other, Graham seemed bursting with joy. "I felt somehow this would be the day you'd make this decision. I'm so happy. Now give me your hands, and we'll pray."

Carrie and Trouble prayed along with Graham, and God's presence entered their hearts. The moment was so encompassing, they cried with happiness. As they hugged each other close, Graham kissed Carrie's forehead lightly.

From the cedars behind them came a harsh, strident voice.

"I must say, this is a pretty picture! My fiancée being kissed by another man like a common woman! Wait until your father hears of this!"

Alfred Rafter, in riding apparel, glared at the three, his face crimson with fury.

Graham faced him boldly. "Before you start calling Carrie names, Mr. Rafter, you should know that we three have been talking about their souls' salvation. Carrie and Travis have just accepted Jesus Christ as their Lord and Savior."

"That is of no importance whatever to me. It only proves how unsuitable a wife she would be. She is capricious, far too fickle to be the wife of Alfred Rafter."

"I'm sorry you have such a low opinion of salvation Mr. Rafter. I hope you never live to regret it."

For a split second, Rafter seemed at a loss. His gaze shifted away from Graham's face. His mouth thinned in a bitter scowl, and he stared belligerently at Carrie.

"You are released from the engagement," he declared "I shall inform your father of this outrageous incident immediately. If I were you, Miss Warden, I should prepare myself for his unfavorable reaction."

With a sweeping glare, he stamped away through the grove of cedars. A few minutes later, they heard his horse's hoofbeats covering the ground en route to the Warden mansion.

Carrie's heart beat so fast she could hardly breathe. What would happen now? Would her father drive her from her home? It was folly to think her mother would stand up for her. And what about Trouble? What would happen to him?

She'd made him part of her rebellion. Surely they would not be so unjust as to condemn him for riding out with her this morning. That would be too cruel. Still, her parents knew how close she and Trouble were. From their point of view, he would be as guilty as she. Carrie began to cry.

"Oh, Carrie, Darling, don't," Graham begged, wrapping her in his arms while Trouble watched in silence. "We'll explain this to your father. We'll make him understand that this was the Lord's business and not a clandestine meeting."

"But it was! Trouble and I came out secretly for the purpose of meeting you, and it has turned out badly. I've taken Trouble down with me. They'll blame him, and he only came along to help me."

"Then let them blame me," Graham protested. "I'm the one at fault. I gave the note to Trouble."

"But I wanted to come," Carrie whispered.

"I'm going with you to your house, regardless of what happens," Graham said.

"Now isn't the time to be scared," Trouble said. "I know Papa will be angry, but Jesus is on our side. He'll make things right. We have to start trusting Him, Carrie."

The shock hit Carrie like a blast of cold water. She was so proud of herself for discovering the spiritual meaning of faith. Of course she had to believe God had the perfect answer!

Graham smiled. "Thanks, Trouble, for taking the right attitude. You're correct. We can depend on the Lord. You're going to be a real soldier for Jesus. I'm proud of you!"

He leaned toward Carrie. "The sooner we go to your home, the better. Rafter will probably make his accusation and leave. It wouldn't do to have your father come looking for us."

She nodded her compliance and allowed Graham to lift her onto Samantha's back. The three of them set out from the grove to cross the field.

sixteen

Once in view of the house, they saw Rafter riding away, down the lane. Papa and Mama were outside, without coats, looking after him.

Carrie broke Samantha's trot and slowed her to walk. "Wait a minute," she said. "This is an important time, and we must make a decision, Trouble. We'll have Graham bowing to Papa the same way we do, and it's not right!" She turned to Graham. "You've done nothing but good for Trouble and me. It's time we pulled ourselves together to decide who is really at fault here.

"Graham, you and Trouble met by accident after you and I had seen each other riding. When Trouble got to know you, he thought you would be better for me than Alfred Rafter; and after a stubborn delay on my part, I began to think so too. You're nearer my age, for one thing, and—" She became aware of Trouble listening intently as he plodded along on Bandy.

"Trouble, you were the first to say that you thought Graham and I liked each other. You were right, and I'm through denying it. Instead, I'm saying it's all right for us to like each other or feel even more than that," she said, trading looks with Graham.

"Papa may be very angry, Trouble. He'll be even angrier

about our becoming Christians, but you and I did the right thing. We must remember that." She reached out and took his hand. "Let's be faithful and trust our Savior to work this out for us."

He squeezed her hand. "I'll stand by you, no matter what happens."

Carrie knew he would.

"I'm proud of both of you," Graham said. He leaned over and placed his hand on theirs. "Dear Lord, be with us as we go forward with faith in You." He sat straight in the saddle. "Let's go."

Before they reached the side gate, Carrie could see tears running down her mother's face.

Papa looked close to apoplexy. "So there you are— you interloper! Leave my property at once! Carrie and Trouble, go to your rooms. I'll deal with you later."

"Mr. Warden, please let me explain. You've not heard the full story. Carrie and Trouble are not at fault here. I—"

"No!" Carrie guided Samantha through the gate, placing Samantha in front of her father. "Papa, for once, you will listen to me."

Carrie felt a strength she'd never known before. She had nothing to be ashamed of. Papa should have been the one to lead her to Christ. Instead, he wanted her rich and socially prominent, without the Lord. She had to show him he was wrong.

"I told you again and again I did not want to marry Alfred Rafter. If I hadn't met Graham this morning, I would have planned to run away. I might even be gone by now. Where, I don't know, but anywhere would have been better than marriage to that miserable man."

Everyone looked at her with startled faces. "Don't be alarmed. Neither Graham nor Trouble knew about this. I was planning my escape when Trouble came to my room last night, and we decided to meet Graham together this morning as he asked.

"Trouble and I have been reading the Bible. We believe that Jesus Christ is the Son of God and that He died as a sacrifice for our sins. At the south pond this morning, we gave our hearts to the Lord. We were crying after we prayed, thanking God for His gracious gift.

"Alfred Rafter came up, saw our arms around each other, and made up his own tale. Our salvation impressed him as little as it has you and Mama. But it is done. Jesus freed me, and I am released from that deplorable engagement."

Carrie heaved a great sigh, and, with her gaze still riveted on her father's face, she asked Graham to help her down. He did, and with his arm around her, they faced her parents.

"There's one more thing you will not like. I am in love with Graham, and there's nothing you can do about that either. He loves me too. I know I'll probably never be welcome in this house again, but that's all right. God is already working out what I'm to do.

"Despite all I've told you, my heart is full of happiness for what happened to Trouble and me today. My dearest wish is that you two will accept Jesus as your Savior also and lead our whole family to do the same. I will pray for that with all my heart."

"It's my prayer too, Mr. Warden," Graham said, holding Mortimer's gaze. "When we've known each other longer, I hope to ask Carrie to be my wife. Together, we will follow God's will to an exciting future. But I'd like nothing better than to have you accept the Lord as well. Your children both love you and Mistress Warden. They did the right thing. They didn't accept Jesus to hurt you. They did it because God chose them."

As Graham talked, Mortimer became less rigid. He looked out over his acreage for a span that seemed like hours to Carrie. Finally he turned his eyes toward them.

"Well, come inside, all of you. We can't keep standing out here in this cold; your mother will take her death."

With nothing more to say, they followed the Wardens, Graham's arm supporting Carrie. She stumbled, and with a sound of concern Graham swept her up to carry her. Mortimer turned and, with a slight shake of his head, continued on. Unseen by the rest, Graham bent slightly and whispered in Carrie's ear, "Good girl!"

Graham led Carrie to her familiar chaise lounge in the parlor and helped her out of her heavy cape. When Mortimer saw the paltry fire, he took another log from the wood box, removed the fire screen, and placed the wood on the coals. Flames licked the log and ignited it to a good blaze.

Mortimer sat in his lean-back chair and waited for Gwendolyn to pour the tea Cook had brought. "Just how do you intend to support my daughter if I consent to this future marriage you claim will happen?"

"I'm a lawyer, Mr. Warden," Graham said. "I have an honorable profession. My prospects are above average, and I expect them to get better when I'm a partner in my uncle's law firm."

Mortimer's eyebrows rose. "Oh-ho! You're going to be a partner in your uncle's law firm. And just when will this dream of yours take place, if I may be so bold?"

Chuckling, Graham picked up Carrie's hand. "Now that I know your daughter, I'll accept my uncle Frederick's offer immediately."

"You've already been offered it, eh?"

"Yes, Sir."

Gwendolyn set the teapot down with a clatter. "Does that mean you'll practice law in Philadelphia?"

Sitting quietly, Carrie was stunned at the panic in her mother's voice. After all the years when her mother could have been close to her, now she was afraid Carrie would go and live elsewhere. How astonishing and how strange that Jesus, on the day she first knew Him, was mending the relationship between her mother and her.

Graham answered in a kind voice. "Yes, Mistress Warden. Philadelphia is a city where a lawyer can attain the income to support a family."

"Pour the tea and serve the muffins, Gwendolyn. Let me talk with this man," Mortimer said roughly.

"Papa! Please don't be rude to Mama!" Carrie cried. "Naturally her questions are going to be different than yours. She loves me. She wants to know what's going to happen to me."

"You think I don't?"

Graham spoke up. "Both of you are thinking of her good. My work is to convince you that I want the same thing and that I'm capable of taking care of your daughter in the future. Carrie is a believer now, and she will find resources within herself that she never had before. I think I can promise you, she will be a very happy young lady."

Mortimer stood, walked to the bay window, and looked out absently. "I don't suppose you'd leave the law and come back here to work for me? I'm going to need an office man soon. My business is growing beyond all expectations. I assure you, the job would pay ample wages to support a family—in the future, that is."

Carrie caught a breath. *Jesus, please don't let Graham agree. Help him know that we need to be independent of my parents. I want to start our life the way You want us to, not the way Papa wants us to; and if we stay here, we might soon be listening to Papa instead of to You. Thank You.*

She had hardly finished her prayer when she heard Graham's strong reply. "I appreciate your offer, Mr. Warden, but the law means a great deal to me. It's all I've ever wanted to do."

"But what good is it? Won't you be bored in such a job after a few years?"

Carrie realized her father was clutching at straws.

Clasping his hands together, Graham sat forward,

resting his forearms on his thighs. "The law covers many areas, Sir. The government of our country is becoming more complex. As I see it, mine is a profession that is wide open. I've worked hard to get where I am, and I intend to work even harder in the future."

Carrie's heart pounded with pride. As she gazed at his handsome face, she too saw that glowing future.

seventeen

In the garden five months after they met, Graham asked Carrie to be his wife. A golden-hued moon shone its light on the couple as they walked together. Beyond the yard, an orchard of fruit trees had put on its spring dressing.

"Carrie, Darling, have you thought about living with me in a place far away from your family?" Graham asked hesitantly.

Carrie grinned. "I've thought of almost nothing else. I have a lot to learn though, Graham. You'll have to be patient. I know little about being the mistress of my own house."

"We'll learn it together. I'll help you," he said, touching a curl on her forehead.

Graham swept her up in his arms and swung her around, her crinoline skirt flying wide. "My sweet love, I predict marriage to you will be like the pot of gold at the end of the rainbow!" He kissed her nose and set her down gently.

"Carrie, I have something for you. When I saw the beautiful full moon tonight, I decided to give this to you out here while we're alone. This is a ring that came from England. I didn't know the lady—she was my mother's aunt. But Mother says she was small and dainty like you, and we all want you to have it. It will be our promise ring of wonderful days to come, together in Christ."

On her finger he slipped a silver band inset with a tiny rose of garnets, emeralds, and seed pearls that sparkled in the moonlight.

"Oh," she whispered. "It's so beautiful." She stood on tiptoe and kissed his cheek. "Thank you, Graham." Her heart full of her own excitement, she reached into her pocket. "I have something for you too. It means more to me than I can tell you."

She took out the tiny gold box. "This is the story you said you'd wait to hear someday. Remember?" Graham nodded. "When I was a little girl, my grandmother Lawrence gave this to me for the romantic man who would one day capture my heart. She asked me to wait for the man I truly loved, and I did.

"Until I met you, I didn't appreciate what a priceless piece of advice she gave me. She promised that God would lead me to the one He had for me. God led me to you, Graham, just as my grandmother said. My true love, here is my dearest legacy as a gift."

Graham opened the box and looked up, questioning. She told him the story of her grandparents' great love. When she finished, his expression spoke to her heart.

"For me the key has deep significance, Graham. My grandmother's love remained steadfast beyond death, and my grandfather's token of affection became a testimony. I had to wait for the man who offered me that kind of love. I had to wait for you. Do you see?"

Graham pulled her to him and kissed her again. "Yes, my love, I see. That you chose to give me the key fulfills a need in my heart also. Thank you for this treasure. It's a precious gift, just as you are."

He smoothed her cheek with his fingertips. "I will be faithful to you, my darling. I will honor you all my life as your grandfather honored your grandmother, and I'll prove my love for you every day I live."

❧

Carrie's feet flew down the steps. "Mama! Mama! It's a letter from Alice Garner in New York! She's coming to my wedding!"

Gwendolyn paused in her arrangement of flowers for the dining room table. "What? She's coming to the wedding?"

"Yes! Isn't it thrilling? I wrote her when Graham asked me to marry him, but I never dreamed she'd be able to attend." Her eyes shining with excitement, Carrie flung herself into a chair and dropped the letter on the table.

Gwendolyn reached for it. "What a wonderful surprise! Do you want her in your room or in one of the rooms close to you? We'll get it ready immediately."

"She's going to stay with her cousin near the church. In fact, she's only going to be here overnight. She and her husband are on their way west. Can you believe it, Mama? Alice, the most independent spirit I ever knew, is married to a preacher!"

Gwendolyn laughed and handed back the letter. "It just goes to show, anyone's life can be turned around by the

Lord. Look what's happening to your father. Whenever he thinks I'm not watching, he reads the Bible, and he never shouts anymore. One night last week, I even caught him praying on his knees in the study. The transformation isn't complete yet, but I declare, I think the man is changing."

Carrie's gaze met her mother's in a bond of understanding. "I know, Mama. I've noticed the change in him too, and how happy it makes me."

Folding Alice's letter, Carrie followed her mother toward her sitting room. Once again, it was time to take up the dreaded task of finishing her wedding trousseau.

❧

"No, Graham Nugent. You can't see Carrie until four o'clock this afternoon," Gwendolyn exclaimed. "The groom must not see the bride until the hour of the ceremony on the day of the wedding!"

Carrie clapped her hand over her mouth to muffle her giggles. Peeking around the corner in the upstairs hall, she could just barely see the scene in the entry below. It was such a strange sight: big, anxious Graham being pushed out the door by her tiny mother in a work dress and apron. Shoulders shaking, Carrie was still laughing when she tripped lightly back down the hall to her room.

"Oh, Graham! How I love you! And today you'll be mine." Humming a little tune, she twirled round and round on the hardwood floor.

"May I have the next number on your dance card, Miss Warden?" Trouble teased, coming out of his room.

"It's about time you woke up," Carrie chided, ruffling his tangled red curls. "Don't you know this is my wedding day? I have chores for you. For one thing, I want you to stay close. Alice and I are forever friends, but you're the one I really depend on."

Trouble frowned. "Yes, I know."

"What's the matter?"

"Nothing you have to worry about."

With her hands on his shoulders, Carrie turned him and pushed him toward her room. He opened the door, and she marched them both inside, her yellow calico dress swirling around her ankles in her abrupt stop.

Hands on her hips, she held his gaze. "All right, no one can hear us now. I want to know what's bothering you. You don't usually stay in bed this late, and I think this is definitely something for me to worry about. 'Fess up now."

Trouble hung his head. "I couldn't risk Papa or Mama sending me off to town on some errand. I wanted to be with you."

"Why, Trouble, I didn't realize—"

"I understand. You've been so busy the past few months, planning for the wedding. It isn't like it used to be when we were together every day."

"Come here," she said and pulled him by the hand to the lounge, where they sat together. "You're not sorry I'm getting married, are you? After all, it's partly your fault." She giggled and, receiving no answer, shook her head. "No, that's not it. It wouldn't be because I'm going away, would it? Because I'll be back often for visits, Trouble."

"But you don't know if that will be possible until you get to Philadelphia and see how you'll live. Graham may have plans or people you'll have to entertain, and there'll be times when you want to come and aren't free to leave." His serious eyes pleaded for her to understand.

Carrie's tears started without warning. He was such a sensitive, wonderful boy. She hadn't given a thought to how her leaving might affect him. Trouble was going to be lonesome.

She wrapped her arms around him. "My sweet brother. You really care, don't you?" She rested her chin on his hair. "All I can tell you is this. I care about you too, and I will come back as often as I can. Besides, you know how much Graham and I love you. Perhaps Mama and Papa will let you come and stay with us for extended visits."

Trouble heaved a sigh. "I sure am glad you said that. I was hoping I'd get to come and stay with you once in awhile."

She nodded, then pointed out the window. Graham, riding slowly toward home, sat straight and tall on Raven's back. "See that man? He's the kindest, most thoughtful man in the world. Of course he'll want you to come stay with us."

Before he reached the crossroads, Graham pulled Raven to a halt, turned, and waved back at the house. Peering through the curtain, Carrie grinned happily.

"That was for me, Trouble. He knew I'd be watching when he left. I always watch, and except for today, I always wave. From now on, I'll never have to wave good-bye again."

When Graham was out of sight, she turned to Trouble. "Go down for your breakfast now. I ate before Graham came. After breakfast, would you bring in the rainwater so I can wash my hair?" He smiled, glad to be helpful, and the smile overwhelmed Carrie. "I love you, Trouble. Right after Graham, you'll always be my best friend."

&

Alice Garner—a taller, thinner version of her former energetic self—arrived as planned. She plunged into the excitement of the wedding, her exuberance adding to Carrie's joy.

"Do you remember what a tomboy I used to be, Carrie?" Alice asked as she slipped on gloves that matched her lavender suit for the wedding.

Carrie laughed. "I remember mostly what an encourager you were. You constantly tried to get me to stand up to Papa."

"I felt sorry for you. You couldn't do anything without asking permission, and it was seldom granted. But all that has changed, I hear."

"Oh, Alice, I'm so glad you and Harold could come to the wedding! I knew you'd have to see Papa to believe the change in him. God has made all the difference in my family, and Graham is the one who turned us toward Him."

"Harold is the same. He loves to bring people to Christ. Some of them will go with us on our westward route tomorrow." She turned smiling eyes to Carrie. "Aren't you glad our men seemed to like each other right away?"

"Yes! And we'll be praying for you as you travel. Will you pray for us too? We're going in opposite directions, but our prayers will keep us close."

"Let's keep the letters going, Carrie, no matter how far apart we are." Alice stood and smoothed the bed cover where she had been sitting. "Much as I hate to, I should get out and let your family have these last hours with you."

The two girls hugged, but Carrie couldn't let go. "Alice, I want to thank you for being my friend when I had none. I think God has kept us close so we can support each other for a lifetime." She stepped back. "Now, don't go too far away. You're part of my family too."

❧

Fluffing her daughter's dress and veil, Gwendolyn talked as she worked. "Carrie, I've not been as good a mother as I should have been. But ever since your father started changing, I've begun to recapture the joy of my own salvation. I was seven years old when I asked Christ into my heart, but I never told a soul. I didn't work at keeping Him close, and I lost my way.

"If only Mortimer and I had all those years back, Carrie, we'd bring you children up as we were meant to. I guess what I'm saying is, I'll try not to fail you after this. Send for me if you need me, please, and I'll be there."

Carrie gathered her mother in her arms. "Thank you, Mama. And, remember, you still have Trouble. Study the Bible with him, and Graham and I will pray for you every day."

Letting her mother go, she asked, "Is Reverend Thomas downstairs, and is everything ready?" Carrie grabbed her hands. "Is Graham here? Please say yes!"

Laughing at her daughter's groundless concern, Gwendolyn kissed her cheek and opened the door. Outside, Mortimer waited, smiling shyly.

His eyes watered at the sight of his daughter. "My, my, Carrie, you're a pretty young lady, and I hardly noticed. Graham is a lucky man." He lowered his head. "No, luck has nothing to do with it. I do believe God meant for you and Graham to be together. I. . .I only wish I could grab back those years of having you close. I'd be a better papa."

Carrie grabbed his hand and held it to her cheek. "Be a better papa to Trouble instead. He's going to miss Graham and me, and he needs your support."

"Yes, well, we're going to do our part. Now, I think we'd better get downstairs. We're holding up the wedding."

At the stairway, Carrie took her father's arm and moved down the steps, her mother following close behind. Eleanor waited in the parlor with Carrie's bouquet of pink roses and her own nosegay of rosebuds. Giving the bride a kiss, she turned and went ahead of the party.

They stepped through the French doors into the garden and waited for the string trio to start the wedding music. The gathered crowd gasped at the sight of Carrie bedecked as a bride.

Carrie's own eyes fixed on Graham. Tall, handsomely tailored, he stood at the altar with Trouble at his side. Dressed in a black jacket with white satin waistcoat and black trousers, he watched Carrie's passage with a look of awed expectation.

Reverend Thomas smiled as the two met, and Mortimer took his seat. The pastor opened his Bible and began the ceremony. Carrie and Graham pledged themselves and their marriage to God.

Without seeing it, Carrie knew that Graham's vest pocket held a tiny pink velvet bag; in it lay Grandmother Lawrence's love gift, Graham's key to her heart.

As the reverend pronounced them husband and wife, Carrie Nugent raised her lips to receive her husband's kiss.

A Letter To Our Readers

Dear Reader:

In order that we might better contribute to your reading enjoyment, we would appreciate your taking a few minutes to respond to the following questions. We welcome your comments and read each form and letter we receive. When completed, please return to the following:

Fiction Editor
Heartsong Presents
PO Box 719
Uhrichsville, Ohio 44683

1. Did you enjoy reading *Two Hearts Wait* by Freda Chrisman?
   ❏ Very much! I would like to see more books by this author!
   ❏ Moderately. I would have enjoyed it more if

   _____

   _____

   _____

2. Are you a member of **Heartsong Presents**? ❏ Yes ❏ No
   If no, where did you purchase this book? _____

   _____

3. How would you rate, on a scale from 1 (poor) to 5 (superior), the cover design? _____

4. On a scale from 1 (poor) to 10 (superior), please rate the following elements.

   ____ Heroine   ____ Plot
   ____ Hero   ____ Inspirational theme
   ____ Setting   ____ Secondary characters

5. These characters were special because?_____

_____

_____

6. How has this book inspired your life?_____

_____

_____

7. What settings would you like to see covered in future
   Heartsong Presents books? _____

_____

_____

8. What are some inspirational themes you would like to see
   treated in future books? _____

_____

_____

9. Would you be interested in reading other **Heartsong
   Presents** titles? ❏ Yes ❏ No

10. Please check your age range:
    ❏ Under 18   ❏ 18-24
    ❏ 25-34   ❏ 35-45
    ❏ 46-55   ❏ Over 55

Name_____

Occupation _____

Address _____

City_____ State_____ Zip_____

BROKEN THINGS

*F*avorite **Heartsong Presents** author Andrea Boeshaar takes us into the world of a woman who courageously faces the failure of her past when she finds a faded photograph of the Chicago cop she once loved. . .but left.

Fiction • 352 pages • 5 ³/₁₆" x 8"

Heart♥ng

Any 12
Heartsong
Presents titles
for only
$30.00*

HISTORICAL ROMANCE IS CHEAPER BY THE DOZEN!

Buy any assortment of twelve *Heartsong Presents* titles and save 25% off of the already discounted price of $3.25 each!

*plus $2.00 shipping and handling per order and sales tax where applicable.

HEARTSONG PRESENTS TITLES AVAILABLE NOW:

__HP179 *Her Father's Love,* N. Lavo
__HP180 *Friend of a Friend,* J. Richardson
__HP183 *A New Love,* V. Wiggins
__HP184 *The Hope That Sings,* J. A. Grote
__HP195 *Come Away My Love,* T. Peterson
__HP203 *Ample Portions,* D. L. Christner
__HP208 *Love's Tender Path,* B. L. Etchison
__HP212 *Crosswinds,* S. Rohde
__HP215 *Tulsa Trespass,* N. J. Lutz
__HP216 *Black Hawk's Feather,* C. Scheidies
__HP219 *A Heart for Home,* N. Morris
__HP223 *Threads of Love,* J. M. Miller
__HP224 *Edge of Destiny,* D. Mindrup
__HP227 *Bridget's Bargain,* L. Lough
__HP228 *Falling Water Valley,* M. L. Colln
__HP235 *The Lady Rose,* J. Williams
__HP236 *Valiant Heart,* S. Laity
__HP239 *Logan's Lady,* T. Peterson
__HP240 *The Sun Still Shines,* L. Ford
__HP243 *The Rising Son,* D. Mindrup
__HP247 *Strong as the Redwood,* K. Billerbeck
__HP248 *Return to Tulsa,* N. J. Lutz
__HP259 *Five Geese Flying,* T. Peterson
__HP260 *The Will and the Way,* D. Pace
__HP263 *The Starfire Quilt,* A. Allen
__HP264 *Journey Toward Home,* C. Cox
__HP272 *Albert's Destiny,* B. L. Etchison
__HP275 *Along Unfamiliar Paths,* A. Rognlie
__HP279 *An Unexpected Love,* A. Boeshaar
__HP299 *Em's Only Chance,* R. Dow
__HP300 *Changes of the Heart,* J. M. Miller
__HP303 *Maid of Honor,* C. R. Scheidies
__HP304 *Song of the Cimarron,* K. Stevens
__HP307 *Silent Stranger,* P. Darty
__HP308 *A Different Kind of Heaven,* T. Shuttlesworth

__HP319 *Margaret's Quest,* M. Chapman
__HP320 *Hope in the Great Southland,* M. Hawkins
__HP323 *No More Sea,* G. Brandt
__HP324 *Love in the Great Southland,* M. Hawkins
__HP327 *Plains of Promise,* C. Coble
__HP331 *A Man for Libby,* J. A. Grote
__HP332 *Hidden Trails,* J. B. Schneider
__HP339 *Birdsong Road,* M. L. Colln
__HP340 *Lone Wolf,* L. Lough
__HP343 *Texas Rose,* D. W. Smith
__HP344 *The Measure of a Man,* C. Cox
__HP351 *Courtin' Patience,* K. Comeaux
__HP352 *After the Flowers Fade,* A. Rognlie
__HP356 *Texas Lady,* D. W. Smith
__HP363 *Rebellious Heart,* R. Druten
__HP371 *Storm,* D. L. Christner
__HP380 *Neither Bond Nor Free,* N. C. Pykare
__HP384 *Texas Angel,* D. W. Smith
__HP387 *Grant Me Mercy,* J. Stengl
__HP388 *Lessons in Love,* N. Lavo
__HP392 *Healing Sarah's Heart,* T. Shuttlesworth
__HP395 *To Love a Stranger,* C. Coble
__HP403 *The Best Laid Plans,* C. M. Parker
__HP407 *Sleigh Bells,* J. M. Miller
__HP408 *Destinations,* T. H. Murray
__HP411 *Spirit of the Eagle,* G. Fields
__HP412 *To See His Way,* K. Paul
__HP415 *Sonoran Sunrise,* N. J. Farrier
__HP416 *Both Sides of the Easel,* B. Youree
__HP419 *Captive Heart,* D. Mindrup
__HP420 *In the Secret Place,* P. Griffin
__HP423 *Remnant of Forgiveness,* S. Laity
__HP424 *Darling Cassidy,* T. V. Bateman
__HP427 *Remnant of Grace,* S. K. Downs

(If ordering from this page, please remember to include it with the order form.)

Presents

Great Inspirational Romance at a Great Price!

Heartsong Presents books are inspirational romances in contemporary and historical settings, designed to give you an enjoyable, spirit-lifting reading experience. You can choose wonderfully written titles from some of today's best authors like Peggy Darty, Sally Laity, Tracie Peterson, Colleen L. Reece, Debra White Smith, and many others.

When ordering quantities less than twelve, above titles are $3.25 each.
Not all titles may be available at time of order.